I0671027

The Long Winter

Kimberly Alderman

ERLEICHDA

Cover art by Janet Guenther

Edited by Joe Kramer

For McCarthy

Published by Erleichda Press

LIBRARY OF CONGRESS CATALOGUING IN
PUBLICATION DATA
Alderman, Kimberly
The Long Winter
p. cm.

ISBN 978-0-9837554-3-2
　　1.　Fiction—Science fiction
　　2.　Fiction—Novels
I. Alderman, Kimberly L., 1979- II. Title

Printed in the United States of America.

Cover art: *Kilaun's Dream* by Janet Guenther (http://www.janetguenther.com/).

When you are sorrowful look again in your heart, and you shall see that in truth you are weeping for that which has been your delight.

- Kahlil Gibran, The Prophet (1923)

1

He awoke knowing that the snow had begun. He could feel it, smell it, and taste it, without so much as opening his eyes or rolling over. It was still September but he'd expected the cold to come early. And with it, the snow.

The old man pulled his blanket up a little further, stealing a few moments of warmth before getting to work. He might have missed his "first snow" deadline, but he still had many chores to take care of before he could focus solely on chopping enough wood to stay warm.

Leif rolled out of bed and slipped his feet into the moccasins that were sitting on the floor. The slippers were sheepskin and duct tape. Mostly duct tape at this point, it seemed. Still better than nothing.

He clambered down the ladder from the loft into the cabin's only room, the journey so routine he scarcely noticed himself doing it. He moved to the window as he pulled another sweater over his head, both fearful and excited to see the world, freshly sanitized by the new snow. The first snow fell like it fell every year – quietly and peacefully, the beauty all the greater for the dangers it brought with it. No matter how much shit the world went through, first snow always felt like rebirth. No matter how ugly or dirty one's surroundings, that first snow was a thing of beauty. Clean. Fresh. New. Even an old man who'd seen as much snow as Leif couldn't deny its effect on him.

The cold trumped the stiffness of an old body freshly out of bed and Leif started moving more quickly the second he felt the air touch his skin. After a few busy minutes, he bustled back inside with an armful of sticks, a handful of fresh eggs, and a freshly emptied bladder. He shuffled across the cold floor to the firebox and knelt down in front of it. He set the eggs gently to the side.

The fire was built with the same care he had used to build his house. He laid two logs next to each other, a few inches apart, and piled the coals left over from the prior night's fire in between them. He gingerly placed a tight bunch of spruce twigs on top of the coals, and a neat little row of small sticks on top of those. Then a layer of medium sticks running snug against one another running the opposite way, finishing up with the thickest sticks on top.

Leif breathed in deep, hunched over, and blew strong and slow between the logs toward the buried coals. He moved his head low to watch the twigs catch from the coals. He blew again to speed them on their way.

He sat on the floor and kept silent vigil until the fire began to crackle and spit.

*

In the time it took Leif to get dressed, the fire had become a roaring blaze. The old can of water sitting on top of the wood stove began to bubble and boil. He tossed a handful of spruce needles into the water and a meager teaspoonful of coffee. He broke the eggs directly on top of the wood stove and used a metal spatula to scrape the congealing goo into a pile.

He ate his eggs and drank his coffee in solitude, sitting at the small table by the window. He knew there was a time when it had been different, but it was hard to believe that there had ever been more than this. How many winters had he spent in the cabin now? How many winters alone?

The first winter, of course, was wonderful. Sam had been with him then. Then there was his second winter, miserable and lonely, when he ran low on food and got sick. Qaniit brought him food scraps from town back then. There were two other winters, one where the wolves got his dogs, and another when Kilaun took over the town. And, in the prior year's winter, nothing happened at all. So Leif calculated this would be his sixth winter.

Only his sixth. It seemed like longer. Would he live this life until he died? Until it killed him? The snow continued to accumulate as he contemplated the life that remained to him. His reverie couldn't last long. He had work to do.

He wasn't sad out there on his own. The quiet suited him. But an old man sometimes wishes for things he hadn't cared about in his younger days. He found himself longing for culture or parties or crowds. He was amused by these longings, knowing that the younger Leif abhorred all that nonsense. Was it a case of the grass being greener? Or had the stillness changed him?

Leif had lived in a city before. It was a legitimate city, with all the fixins: skyscrapers and housing projects, art museums and graffiti, hero capitalists and homeless junkies living under bridges. Humanity, in concentrated form, and he'd been a part of it as much as any of the rest of them.

That life felt like someone else's. It felt like a story he'd read. He looked around his tiny cabin and saw there wasn't a shred of that life left. When Leif arrived in Alaska – well, what was called Alaska then – he had little with him. He and Sam built the cabin with hand tools and tears, rushing to beat that first winter that would ultimately take her from him.

Leif got choked up thinking of her. It hadn't been like that for a while, but it happened more frequently as the years passed. He brought his campclean plate over to the counter. He used a little of the water on the stove to wash it over a bucket. He slipped the plate into his only cabinet and threw some beans in an iron pot on the stove to cook for later.

After gearing up, Leif went outside to start on the chores that patiently awaited him.

2

By the time the snow started, Qaniit had already left town. She, too, had known winter would come early. It seemed like every year it came earlier than it did the last.

The road she walked on was barely a road anymore. The vegetation held back, save for the occasional alder, but the surface was so rough and rutted that no cart could be used. A dog followed reticently behind her.

"Come on," she cooed, "You'll have to hold up better than that." The dog picked up speed and trotted up close to her hand, but fell behind again soon enough. Qaniit hoped he would continue to follow, but walked at a pace that could get her out and home before dark.

She knew the road well, though she hadn't traveled it in years. No one went to visit Leif anymore. It was not worth the trouble that it brought.

She wrinkled her nose wishing it did not have to be that way. She used to enjoy his company. He was good at listening, and his outsider's perspective could be a refreshing break from the timidity and groupthink one encountered in town.

A cold wind blew and the snow stuck. Qaniit pulled the neck closed on her bulky coat. It could keep her warm in colder weather than this, but she still looked forward to the warm fire Leif would have going. Hopefully. The thought that she didn't even know if he was alive tried to drive its way into her consciousness but she blotted it from her mind. Thinking that way wasn't going to help anything and she'd already chosen her course of action.

Qaniit was a small woman, distinctly petite, but her personality outpaced her size. She moved her little legs quickly, to keep warm and so the dog would have to walk fast enough not to lose interest. She did not look at him when he whimpered.

The aspens lining the road were noticeably taller than she'd remembered. She came to an old, gutted trailer that had been there since time immemorial. The roof had collapsed, probably in the previous winter and, from the looks of it, the entire structure would soon follow. Just another remnant of what came before yielding to a new reality.

Qaniit stared at it as she passed. She thought of her body going through that same process. It would eventually succumb to the world, too. She had been so tired lately.

Her life in the village was not exactly bad. There was safety and security. Certainly, there was no woman in a better position than she. But safety and security were only as valuable as the life they protected, and hers was entirely devoid of enjoyment. Kilaun no longer gave her any affection, and he was growing increasingly difficult to handle. She found herself retreating into her own mind, thinking more and more about the past.

"A hollow shell," she said aloud, without realizing she was speaking until the sound reached her ears.

Winter might be better. She would have more free time to take walks, and could maybe even disappear for a day here and there to be alone with her thoughts. Qaniit did not mind caring for the townspeople but sometimes, when she looked at them, she saw animals instead of brethren.

The snow continued to fall, obscuring the road. She trod carefully. The dog was lagging behind. She pulled the basket she was carrying into the crease of her elbow so she could slip her hands and lower arms inside the generously cut sleeves of her coat.

Qaniit walked noiselessly, trying not to think of what trouble she might get in for having gone missing. Instead, she watched the snow and trees, wishing she could spend more time among them.

*

By the time she came to the boggy clearing that marked the turn to Leif's cabin, Qaniit was tired and hungry. She ambled up the unbroken trail through ankle-high snow. The dog cried from a ways behind her. She called, "Come on, boy! You can do it!" with false enthusiasm. She suspected her weariness showed through.

She walked up the narrow path, which had healthy willow starts poking out of the snow right in the middle of it. With each step, the thoughts of the consequences of her trip faded and the guilt she felt for not having visited sooner grew. Leif was out there alone.

The hood on Qaniit's coat hung down over her eyes, and she watched where she stepped. She saw a barn out of the corner of her eye and lifted her head. Further down the road was Leif's cabin, well maintained given the circumstances, with smoke coming out of the chimney. With the first sign of life, the tension she had not noticed before relaxed. There had been no guarantee he would even be alive.

She half-ran to the cabin and rapped on the door. No answer. She knocked again, and nothing. She leaned off the side of the stoop to look in the window, but could not quite reach.

"What's that for?"

Leif's voice bellowed from just a few feet behind Qaniit and it startled her. She lost her grip on the windowsill and tumbled into the snow.

"Thanks, Leif," she mumbled, rolling onto her side to look at him. Her hood fell back and she shot him a look of annoyance.

"I'm not the one who was peeping," he responded.

Qaniit did not bother to answer, and struggled to her feet. Her hands were cold from the fall and she stamped her feet on the porch to get the snow off her boots.

"What's that for?" Leif asked, nodding toward the basket. It was the same basket she used to bring him food in all those years ago, albeit worse for the wear. Just like Leif. And Qaniit herself, most likely.

She just looked at him. He was older, but still kind, in a gruff sort of way. "It's good to see you, too," she said.

Leif looked around and then down the path. She followed his gaze to the dog skulking near the barn.

"What's wrong with it?" he asked.

Qaniit sighed. There never was small talk with Leif. "Quills."

He looked her in the eyes and asked, "Came out here for quills?"

Qaniit looked at him, locked his gaze, and set her jaw. She knew he couldn't turn her away.

"Fine. Bring it in."

3

Libby was angry as hell when the first snowflake fell. Were they going to leave her in this pisshole to freeze and starve to death? She snorted in contempt for their supposed New Order. "Order, my ass," she grunted. She sat up and pulled the wool blanket around her shoulders. The snow fell into her cell through the bars in the high window.

She breathed deep and prepared to wail and carry on like she had done every morning. She had nothing else to do, and the hard work got her a little warmer. Why she had agreed to come up to such a god-forsaken piece of shit wasteland Libby could not remember.

Since her antics had been so persistent and loud, Libby had been moved to a cell with four solid walls, save for the tiny window which should have been closed up by now, and a door with just enough space underneath to shove food and supplies through.

They had given her a pair of cold weather boots, so at least her feet were warm and clean. She could still feel the cold creep into her feet from the dirt floor, though.

As she sat there thinking about what kind of foul things she might shout to those bastards and anyone who could hear, she looked out the window and saw the snow falling. A quiet came over her, so she stopped thinking, and just watched.

Libby had not seen snow in a long, long time. Since she was a young child. She tried to think of whether she really remembered snow or if it was just a dream.

It felt like a dream. There, wrapped in a blanket, *imprisoned* (just to think the word, she shuddered in anger), watching the snowfall one flake at a time. The snow looked so delicate. Such a peaceful thing.

Her thoughts were interrupted when the door swung open and hit the wall behind it. She did not even turn her head. She just watched the snow.

"Aren't you going to scream and yell?" a voice asked.

"Not today," she replied, "I'm tired."

"Are you cold?"

"I don't know," she mumbled.

"I can cover the window."

"No!" she jerked around to look at the man speaking to her. She had not seen this one before. He was a large man, doughy, but with a gentle look on his face, like he might be mentally impaired. She regained herself and asked, "Will you leave it open for today?"

He shrugged. "You like snow?"

She faded out again and looked back at the whiteness.

"It's pretty," the large man said. And, with that, he closed the door and left Libby to herself.

4

"Where is SHE?" Kilaun roared as he plowed through the kitchen, knocking the maid out of his way.

The cook knocked the back door closed with her backside, and dumped an apron full of potatoes on the counter. The maid recovered her balance and stuttered a nonsensical response. Kilaun fumed and the cook interjected casually. "With respect, Sir, she would hardly be hiding in here."

Someone giggled. "If she were, I'd put her to work." Chena had known him a long time, and refused to respond to oversized temper tantrums, fearsome though they were.

Kilaun huffed and stormed out of the room.

Sila whispered, "Did she go to the toe?" The cook swung a wooden spoon and hit the girl. A sharp cry escaped her, but the emergence of another was forestalled by the maid's quick hand.

The maid looked nervously at Chena, who had taken to quickly chopping the potatoes. The little girl Sila sulked while she went back to picking the eyes clean on the potatoes.

When the cook was done chopping, she said, flatly, "Tali, I need your help in the root cellar."

The maid brushed off her hands and murmured, "Of course."

Chena took down a large pot and dropped it on the counter. She turned to the girl, who sat dejected by the potatoes, and commanded, "Start some water to boil."

With a look of resignation on her face, Sila reached for the pot. The two women left the room.

*

"Close both doors," Chena huffed, lumbering down the narrow hall of the root cellar.

Tali looked behind her, out of the door, as she closed it. The town was quiet with first snow. She grunted slightly as she lifted the heavy wooden door to pull it tight into the frame.

Chena lit the lamp as Tali got the second door.

"Where's Qaniit?" the cook challenged.

Tali averted Chena's stare just long enough to get smacked across the face.

Tali did not cower this time. She was tired of cowering. "You don't scare me."

"Yes, you are," thought Chena, and it brought a bit of a smile to her face. The cook was right, Tali was scared of her. Chena refused to treat the girl any differently than she'd treat anyone else. Too many people coddled Tali because of the way she looked. Chena did not buy into that system. *You work or you get worked.* A pretty face and figure made no exception to that rule. Not for Chena, at least.

"Disloyalty will get your throat slit," Chena hissed.

"Not today it won't." Tali said, hoping she sounded bolder than she felt.

Chena stared at her, and Tali cracked, like she always did. "She went up to the glacier toe."

The cook was almost glad that Tali was such a traitor. The townspeople, including Qaniit, opened up to Tali in a way they never opened up to her.

Chena sputtered, "I should have killed that damned dog myself."

"Gun's a good dog," Tali whispered, sitting down on an old milk crate. She pushed at some dirt with her foot.

"Not worth the trouble it'll cause if Kilaun finds out. We could've used the meat anyway."

"You know he'd be too tough," Tali said.

The cook sighed and sat on a bucket in the other corner of the dimly lit room. It was warmer in the cellar than it was outside. Winter was early this year. Again. Chena dropped her head back and rested it on a wooden roof support.

"Tough as shit alive, tough as shit dead," the cook said in a half-hearted joke.

Tali nodded her head. "You think the boys'll bring back some sheep?"

"It got cold quick. I'll be satisfied if they bring back themselves."

The women sat quietly, both wondering if Qaniit would return by nightfall.

5

Leif hunched over Gun, looking carefully to see that he got all the quills out. The dog was laid out on the only table in the room, and he twitched and kicked occasionally. Leif swabbed the dog's face and neck with whiskey as a finishing touch. Perhaps the dog preferred higher-grade stuff, as the physician's homemade vintage made Gun squirm even more.

Leif crossed the room to sit with Qaniit by the stove. They had not spoken for the two hours it took him to remove the quills. He offered her the flask. She declined. He went ahead and took a swig himself. It tasted like shit, but it was strong enough.

"They wanted to kill him," she explained, gesturing to the dog.

"Worst case I've ever seen," he said. "Not worth killing over, though."

"I brought you some food. Not too much good though."

"Just like the old days," he said, but he realized his voice sounded bitter.

"I'm sorry I haven't visited."

"You don't owe me anything, Lisa." He tried not to sound like he was emphasizing the last word in the sentence, but it didn't really work.

"Don't call me that."

"This isn't Kilaun's domain."

"Still."

"You're under his complete control. How can you stand it? Why do you stand it?"

"Where else would I go?" she said, half pleading, half yelling. "I'm not about to…." Her eyes had been in the midst of a sweep across the cabin when she halted her sentence, but her meaning was just as obvious as if she'd finished. The effect was the same. He knew what she meant. And she knew he knew. It produced an awkward silence.

Leif found her changed. Was it just a couple more years on the tally, or life with Kilaun that had brought it about? Age subdues everyone eventually. It seemed the same could be said of Kilaun, and it usually didn't take as long.

"I guess I wouldn't mind the horses," she said.

He chuckled. She used to love to ride the horses.

"You still have them?"

"Buck and Shadow, yup. Lucky died last year," he said. Lucky was a good horse. Lucky was the horse that carried him up to this country. "And Shadow's pregnant."

It was his turn to regret speaking. Her eyes darted to the floor the instant he mentioned the pregnancy. He knew she'd lost a child. Still not over it, apparently.

After a few moments of silence, he settled on an appropriate change in subject matter. "Is there news of outside?"

Qaniit's mournful expression fell away. "There's a new government. Minarchists, this time."

"All governments are the same."

"Oh, I thought I'd left Kilaun back at the village."

That barb stung. Leif didn't trust himself to respond civilly so he kept his mouth shut. Kilaun might claim that philosophy but it didn't change what his actions in the village really constituted. What Kilaun called a "social structure" would've been recognized by anyone else as what it was, a fucking government. Just another government.

Qaniit continued, "They sent an emissary."

"I'm sure that went well."

"She's locked up. There'll be an assembly."

Leif rolled his eyes. An "assembly." One that would conveniently affirm Kilaun's decision on the matter. Just like all past assemblies had, just like all future ones would. Window dressing, they called it. Everyone could have his or her own opinion, as long as it agreed with Kilaun's.

"His brother came up from the Pass last month. It's pretty bad out there, I guess."

Leif raised an eyebrow. Qaniit was quiet.

"You won't make it back before dark," he warned her.

"I won't turn into a pumpkin."

Leif had a vague memory of what that used to mean, but it wasn't quite coming to him.

"What will you tell him?" he asked.

"We don't talk enough for him to ask me. I'm sure he's having a fit about it now, though. He'll get angry enough that he won't even ask."

Leif looked at her and remembered their first meeting. On a cruise, or so the joke had gone. A refitted cruise ship, with close to ten thousand people on board. Huddled masses. The only food was what one brought, and Qaniit did not have enough. She was frail in her body, but strong in her spirit. She confided her regret that she had killed a man to get on board. He gave her some food anyway.

"Do you ever think about living in town?" she asked quietly.

His head jerked up to her eyes immediately. His glare was answer enough.

The dog stirred and Leif went to help him off the table. He set the dog gently on the floor, and the dog just laid back down with his eyes half open.

Qaniit went to the counter. "I need to empty the basket."

"He's not ready to walk."

"He's better suited than before."

Leif helped her empty the basket. They pulled out potatoes, cabbage, rhubarb, and bread, piling them on the counter.

"Tali made the bread for you."

"Taliriktug?" he asked, surprised.

"She's a woman now, Leif. She works in our house."

Leif pressed his lips together, angry. He felt like Kilaun had recreated all the worst aspects of the old world, including injustice. Taliriktug was the daughter of a good friend of his, an educated, respected man, and she was an intelligent girl, and she should not be relegated to serving some narcissistic glorified tribal chief.

"She's treated well," Qaniit reassured him.

"And you?" he quipped.

She took her empty basket, and helped the dog onto his feet. His legs were still wobbling, and he looked confused.

"We have to go," she said. And, with that, she and the dog left the cabin.

Just like that. No goodbye. Maybe it was the last conversation Leif would ever have with another person. He stood in the doorway and watched the woman and the dog go. Of course he wondered what it was like to live in town. To have conversations. To see people. Seeing children grow up. Seeing your peers grow old.

No matter the comforts, it wasn't worth it. It couldn't be worth it. His life was harsh, but it was his. It was enough. It had to be.

6

"Kilaun?" Chu called, knocking on the door twice.

No answer.

Chu let himself into his brother's room, but it was not empty. Kilaun lay in bed with a woman. Chu had seen her before in the kitchen.

"What do you want?" Kilaun hissed.

"I—sorry. Thought you were gone," Chu stammered.

"What. Is. It. Talk or get the hell out, Chu."

Chu stood there, struck dumb by a mixture of intimidation, the mystery of sex, and a vague understanding that he wasn't supposed to be there.

"Maybe Qaniit…you should…," Chu stammered, looking anywhere and everywhere but the bed.

"Shut up and get…!" Kilaun roared. "The way she…!" His rage wouldn't allow him to finish a sentence, but the tone was clear enough. In his outburst, he'd sat up in bed. He had scars that Chu had not seen before. Kilaun breathed deep with his eyes closed then tried again, "Go. Please, just go."

Chu fled back into the corridor. He knew he had to leave but couldn't think of any place to go to. So he just went.

The snow had stopped. It was dusk. Chu walked through the town square aimlessly, looking at the houses, hints of fluttering dim light visible in some of the windows. He'd been here less than two weeks. Everything was foreign.

There was food. There was no violence. He was with his brother. But, somehow, he didn't feel any safer than he had before.

Kilaun was mean. But having somebody mean was better than having nobody at all, and that's how it was at the Pass. The few families left out there were not doing well. He wondered if Kilaun would invite them to come live here. Chu would've liked that.

The trip from the Pass had taken three days and had been hard on Chu. He still felt a little pain in his feet. He had tried to stick to the sides of the river, at the bottom of the cliffs, but when the vegetation got too thick he had to walk on the ice. When he had finally arrived in town, hungry and tired, he was happy to see Kilaun. Even when his brother was mean he was still his brother and that would not change.

Chu found himself on the other side of town from Kilaun's house and everything was quiet, now dark. The stars were peeking through the clouds. Chu heard something rustling on the hill that sounded like people. He could see nothing.

"Who's there?" Chu shouted. Chu was a little afraid to be yelling out into the darkness, but he was a big man and was smart enough to know that other people saw him as a big man.

"Chu?" a female voice whispered.

"I'm Chu!" he declared loudly. His bravado sounded fearless, even if a bit labored.

A woman emerged from the brush. Qaniit. Chu liked Qaniit.

"Hello, Chu."

A dog walked out of the woods and smelled Chu's hand carefully. "Hello, doggie," he said. Chu liked dogs. Dogs were never confusing.

"Chu! You need a coat. It's too cold out to walk around like that."

He looked down and saw he was wearing inside clothes, and that must be why he felt so cold. He forgot even to put boots on, and his house slippers were wet.

"Kilaun is mad," he said, staring at and squishing his slippers.

"Oh, of course he is," she said, shrugging. "He's Kilaun." She contorted her face into an exaggerated grumpy frown and was rewarded for her performance by a grin from Chu.

"I'm cold," she said. "Let's get inside."

*

Qaniit pushed the back door open and found the kitchen empty. She hurried Chu and the dog in behind her before pushing the door shut. The wood stove was still going, and the glow from the fire filled the room through a glass door. The dog collapsed right in front of it, and did not even eat or drink before falling fast asleep.

"Is he okay?" Chu asked.

"Oh, he'll be fine."

Chu sat down on a stool and put his elbows on the counter. He watched Qaniit set a basket and her gloves near the stove. She struggled to get her ice-caked fur coat off. "Are you okay?" he asked, curiously.

Qaniit hung the coat on a nail. "Oh, I'll be fine, too." She half-smiled when she looked at Chu. She was flush, her face red from the cold. She stamped her feet a little before pulling her boots off.

Chu had not talked much with his brother's wife and had not noticed how pretty she was. Chu had a woman once, some years ago, but he could not keep her. He wondered why his brother did not talk much to this one. She was pretty and seemed strong, which Chu thought was good. She lifted a log with one small hand and threw it in the fire.

"How are you liking it here, Chu?"

"It's OK, I guess," he responded.

"Do you think you'll stay?" she asked, pouring water from a bucket into a pot.

"Maybe." Then, after a pause, he added, "There's nowhere else to go."

She muttered, "I know what you mean," just loudly enough for him to hear. But she was facing away, so he did not think that was for him, and he did not respond. She put the pot of water on the stove.

Chu's clothes were wet so she told him to put them by the stove.

He put his boots and sweater in the little space that was left near the stove. He made sure not to wake the dog, which looked dead. Qaniit made some tea and gave him a cup. He thought about how kind she was. She found some bread left over from dinner and set it on the counter.

"Let's get my secret stash," Qaniit said, opening a drawer, reaching far inside to a hidden part. She pulled out a jar of jelly.

"Is that...? Jelly!" He was practically vibrating with excitement. Jelly. He hadn't had that in years.

"Chena made it for me last year, and I've been hoarding it," she said. "What do you say we finish it up now?"

Chu smiled wide and shook his head happily.

7

Kilaun could see the entire valley from where he stood on the ridge. It was so white now. The first snow had stayed, and it was followed by several more. He welcomed it as protection. No one came in during winter, and no one went out.

In one direction, Kilaun could see his town, several miles away. It was so tiny. It seemed so insignificant from all the way up there. But the town was him and he was the town, even when he was far away.

In the other direction was the glacier. The icefalls looked so big, they dwarfed the mountains behind them.

He saw the glacier toe below him, and thought about the one that lived on the other side of it. That man had been in the area as long as Kilaun had. He wondered if the man was still alive out there, alone with those horses. It was selfish, to live like that, contributing to nothing but your own existence. The man had skills. He could've chosen to make the village stronger, safer, better. But instead, he lived only for himself.

Kilaun was both envious of and disgusted by the lack of responsibility inherent in that other life. Kilaun didn't have freedom, but at least he had built something that would outlast him in this world. The safety and security of the group had never mattered to Leif before and they probably never would. That's how some people were. A shame though, a man with Leif's skills and abilities would be an enormous asset, if only he could be bothered to think of someone besides himself.

Kilaun ceremoniously spat into the snow.

Behind him was the large ridge that sheltered the town from the wild. Now, it was nothing but whiteness and shadows and highlights and wonder. In the summer, it would be much different. The men would spend time hunting in those hills.

This was his place to be alone. To be alone and think. A brief respite from all the burdens Kilaun had to carry.

Yet, here, where he supposedly did his best thinking, was the only place where he managed to not think about everything that was wrong. Like his wife. He would do anything for her, yet there was no gratitude for the burdens he bore every moment of every day. She didn't even seem to have a fondness for him, though she liked his brother well enough. His poor, helpless brother. Yet another burden, piled upon Kilaun's shoulders.

Helpless as Chu was, at least there was loyalty in him. And at least his following Qaniit around like a puppy kept him out of Kilaun's hair.

The outsider. There was no good solution to that problem. Yes, of course they'd have an assembly, and Kilaun would have to save the townspeople from their own stupidity. The burden was on him, same as always.

There could be no risking the Minarchy learning of the town's location and resources, so the woman could not be released. Outsiders would not be able to bear the thought of a community of plenty, with food, with children, with peace, and they'd bring the hammer down and destroy all of it. Kilaun wasn't strong enough to fight them. Not yet, at least.

It would be what happened at the Pass all over again. He'd gotten the story from Chu so it was far from clear just what had gone on. But, it was clear enough that Kilaun knew he didn't want it happening to his people.

His people. And, yet, he could sense the disloyalty. He had given everything for them, he continued to give everything every day. They were alive only because of his efforts, and there was no better place to live for hundreds of miles. Hell, maybe thousands. If they could truly understand Kilaun's vision for the place, it'd be different. Maybe they'd start working, start caring, building, making things happen. He'd still bear the brunt of it. But couldn't they shoulder just a little more?

It would be simpler living alone in the woods. Food and clothing and shelter for one. But everyone would die, die for his selfishness. Kilaun stayed to protect them and they never ceased to punish him for it.

He looked forward to the day when their society would be strong, when fear of succumbing to the psychological illness affecting the outside was long past. But it was not that day yet.

Kilaun did not want to govern the people of his small town. He did not want to be a commander, or a chief, but that is what he had become. It was what the people and the place needed in a terrifying time. It was what they had made him.

In the outside, when things fell apart, the humans resorted to violence and savagery. A decade had passed, but they were not yet done with their war.

A war against whom? Against what? Themselves. The earth.

So they kept on killing each other, hoping for what Kilaun did not know. For a few more days of survival?

They looked to government to save them, and this was their mistake. They must save themselves, first. That is why Kilaun rejected all the proposed governments. They were flawed, every one of them, because they put responsibility in an institution instead of on individual people. And they collapsed, every one of those governments, always, just like Kilaun said they would. They lasted six months, sometimes a year, but no longer. Stability in government would not be possible until stability could be found in the small communities, and in the people themselves.

This woman, the prisoner, Kilaun would not kill her. He was not a savage like those humans Outside. His ancestors would not permit it. He wished he knew more about them. But he would also not let her run free to her government, and invite the Outsiders to rape and pillage and destroy all that he had built. He knew there must be a solution, and he needed to search his soul and the souls of his people to find the answer.

I will call the assembly.

8

Qaniit was drawing when Kilaun returned. She heard him thundering down the hall well before the door burst open.

She continued drawing and said nothing. He, too, remained silent, but she could feel him looming over her. She could feel his gaze – accusing, angry, menacing.

"Maybe if I were a half-wit you could be bothered to acknowledge me. But I'm just your husband, no need to pay me any mind, is there, Qaniit?"

"Hey," she managed. She still hadn't looked up from her drawing.

He was shuffling around doing something or other, but she didn't want to lose their unspoken battle by looking up, so she continued her work.

"I want to have a child," he said.

She was silent for a few moments as she examined her work, then casually replied, "I'm drawing."

Kilaun reached past her and snatched the drawing away. She offered no objection or resistance.

"A horse. It's a horse."

"You certainly are the observant one." She couldn't help herself.

"Mocking me? Why are you mocking me? You give me nothing but grief. I want something different. I want a child."

Qaniit reached across and took the drawing back from him. It wasn't that he didn't like horses. It was more that he didn't like her liking horses.

On her way back from Leif's place last month, she had stopped in his barn. His horses' power and grace took her breath away.

Buck was the horse that had carried her up to this place. She had cried when she saw him again at Leif's.

"I want to get you a horse," her husband said, staring at her.

She looked up at him for the first time since he came in. "Why's that?" she asked suspiciously.

"It will give you something to do other than spend time with my brother," he said sharply.

She went back to her drawing. Kilaun was such a jealous man. She was sure he was fuming about the time she spent with Chu. She did not care. His jealousy made him look ridiculous. "Well, I don't know where you'll find a horse anyway."

"That man up near the toe. He had horses."

It made Qaniit nervous to hear her husband talking about Leif. She owed Leif a good deal. She repaid that debt by keeping him and her husband apart. "I'm sure he's dead by now," she cooed.

"He might not be," Kilaun said sternly.

She changed the subject. "How was your trip to the ridge?"

He got up and put on his nightclothes. "There are lots of wolves this year." He started getting ready for bed.

Qaniit continued to draw.

"They're killing off the hares," he said.

"Fine by me," she said. Those hares got into the gardens in the summer and ate a good half of the crop, including all the peas, which particularly annoyed her. And hares weren't any good for eating, either. They did eat them of course, better than nothing, but they were nothing like the rabbits her father would bring home when she was a child. Those were delicious. She salivated just to think of them.

"I'm going to call the assembly."

She stopped drawing. "The woman in the jail?"

He nodded.

"She's not looking too good, Kilaun."

"I know," he snapped. "That's why I'm calling the assembly. I'll resolve this issue one way or the other."

Qaniit looked at her husband. She knew he would not kill the woman, but was not sure he would not let her die. He was so protective of this town, of his creation, that he might just let a person starve to death to keep it safe. Qaniit hoped that did not become necessary.

"Ten days?" she asked.

"Ten days," he huffed. And with that, he climbed into bed, leaving his wife to draw her horses in peace.

9

The door to Libby's cell swung open and the big man stood there. She was sitting on the bed, picking at her hands. They were cracking and dirty.

"I have hot water for you," he said.

She stood up to take the pot from him. She saw him frown when her reaching exposed her wrist. She pulled back and covered it up. She knew she was too thin.

"Are you getting enough food?" he asked.

"Yes," she said quietly. Libby hunched over the pot much like an animal. She washed her face, her arms. She felt like an animal, taking the morsel of hot water and savoring it. "Why are you smaller?" he asked, curiously.

She did not answer. He stood waiting, and said, "It's cold."

She saw him look at the window. "Please don't cover it," she asked, desperately.

The big man cocked his head. "Okay."

He left her with the water.

Libby was too cold, but she had grown attached to that window. Her little window to a world. Not *the* world, not even *her* world, but *a* world. All she could see from her bed was the snow falling and the stars. If she stood, she could see the top of a nearby spruce tree, now iced with snow.

As she washed herself, Libby calculated how long she had been there. Forty-six days, she thought. Or was it more?

At first the worst thing about being locked up was the boredom. She had nothing to do. Once or twice someone had ended up in the next cell over for a few days, but conversation from window to window was limited.

To entertain herself, Libby had sometimes put her bare feet on the dirt floor and see how long she could hold them there. The way the cold crept in, it did not even feel like cold. It felt like ache, crawling up her feet, then ankles, then calves.

There was a woman who brought food sometime. Libby had never seen her face. She seemed kind though the door, though. She sounded young, maybe fearful. This woman would talk to her a little bit, just a little, but enough that Libby looked forward to when she might visit. It was better to hear her soft steps than the click clacking of the cook's shoes and just the clink of a tray on the ground.

The boredom ceased to matter after a while. Her body's response to the cold and hunger was a sort of waking slumber. It was shutting down everything that wasn't entirely necessary for survival, including her emotions.

Libby finished washing and put the pot by the door. She pulled her clothes straight and lay down on the bed. She watched the surface of dirty water in the pot. It still steamed slightly.

She drifted between sleep and wakefulness, though never far from the border between them. This was how Libby spent most of her time and she knew this was a sign that her body was in poor condition.

Libby had done well for herself on the Outside. She wondered if she would go back, but without particularly caring. Going back had been all that mattered to her when she'd first been locked up. Tears sprang from her eyes thinking of all she'd left behind, thinking of dying here in this dismal and frigid hell. Caring required too much energy of her at this point.

Before, Libby had a job. It barely paid, but it was a job. People envied her for that. And she felt like she was working toward something worthwhile. The people had wanted a government for years. Some had tried, but with no success. Each attempt at a government was shortly thereafter damned by a coup, a wild mob, or a political implosion. The rapid succession of failed governments was demoralizing. Still, she'd felt there was hope for the Minarchy, back when she'd had the capacity to hope.

All people really wanted was safety. They wanted protection from violence. They wanted to let their children outside. They wanted to walk at night without weaponry. The Minarchy assured them that, and no more. It was ideal because of its simplicity.

Libby grasped that the people in this town had perceived her as a threat. There was a chief-type man, Kilaun, who seemed to be in charge, and who seemed exactly like the sort of person you'd expect to be in charge in a place like this. The caveman with the biggest club. Libby had come as an emissary, not a warrior. What could she possibly do to them by herself?

But who knew what horrors these people had endured before Libby's arrival? Who knew if she would have behaved any differently than they did? Her anger had faded along with everything else.

When she had set out, seemingly in another lifetime, she hadn't been alone. When her traveling partner fell ill, Libby set out on her own in search of help and had stumbled right into the village. She had no idea whether he had survived. Once she realized the town commander would keep her captive, she could not give away her partner's location. It had been so long, though. If he had survived, wouldn't he have come for her? She wasn't thinking about it that often anymore. Now she just watched the snow fall.

Libby had been overjoyed when she had first seen the village. She'd expected it to be her salvation. Now she realized it was more likely her death.

*

In Libby's half-sleep, images of her old life came to her. Her son was foremost among them, but frivolous things appeared, too. The man teacher she'd had a crush on when she was twelve. A garden that she'd once planted and had to leave before harvest time.

Lumbering steps snapped her back into awareness and she knew the big man was coming back. Her eyes blinked open when he opened the door, but betrayed no sign of alertness or curiosity. His eyes fell upon her for an instant, causing her to imagine the sight she must have presented. He took the pot and set a folded blanket on the floor by the door, then left without a word.

To get the blanket meant exposing herself to more cold. And she was so tired. She meant to get it but couldn't quite bring herself to spring into motion. She could get it the next time food arrived. That way, she wouldn't have to get up twice. There, it was decided. She shut her eyes.

Libby drifted back into sleep, and had a dream about the old days, when she had a husband and a television.

10

Chena took the back way home after work hoping she'd less likely encounter someone who would try to make demands on her time. She wanted nothing more than to go home and collapse by the fire. She knew she'd better fry some potatoes first, but that was the only concession her exhaustion would allow.

She was immediately annoyed when her cabin came into sight. The pile of wood to the side of the door would not last more than two days. She had told Soapy that he needed to chop more wood that day. Chopping wood was not too much to ask for all she did. Yet, clearly no firewood had been added to the pile. It was a disheartening thing to return home to after a long and tiring day of work.

What is so difficult about chopping wood? You get the log, you split it, and you stack it. It's not like trying to cook for the chief of the village, preparing meals that please His Finickiness and to further coordinate two households, your own and a mess of someone else's. Is it so difficult? He has to contribute so little and yet it's still too much?

Her son was called Soapy. Sometimes it seemed like he never did right. Chena would have to babysit him into chopping wood the next morning or else chop it herself, in which case Soapy might as well find himself another place to live. She did not need another useless mouth to feed, no thank you.

Work or get worked.

The cabin was dark and cold, without a single coal in the stove. Soapy had been gone all day. Probably chasing women around.

When will that boy learn it ain't gonna happen? He should be embarrassed, carrying on like a dog in heat.

And, the worst of it, he kept after that silly maid, the one that Kilaun took when he was angry with his wife. There was no way in hell Chena was going to tell Soapy the girl was Kilaun's lover – that boy had the biggest damn mouth. He'd probably get her throat slit in a matter of hours. Not that the girl seemed good for anything but what Kilaun used her for anyhow.

Chena kneeled on an old hide trying to get the fire going when she heard Soapy stamping the snow off his boots on the porch. Sure enough, he fell into the room a minute later, discombobulated as always.

"Night, ma!"

"Night, yourself. Now where's my firewood?"

"Oh, ma, there's enough for three more days. And look what I got!" Soapy held up a few scrawny rabbits and a squirrel, smiling as proud as a 12-year-old boy who'd just brought home a moose. Chena might not have the energy to stay mad at him, but she sure wasn't gonna let him know that.

He needs to know to do what I tell him, and that's that.

"Dog food?" she snipped.

The grin fell from Soapy's face and he lowered his trophies and head. He kicked off his boots and dropped the animals on the table. Chena figured she would use the rabbits tonight and the squirrel in the morning. She'd rather have some sheep, but the boys didn't make it far enough up the mountain this year. Something about their camp stove giving out. Chena suspected some combination of laziness and incompetence based on her knowledge of the group.

Soapy's face was devoid of expression as he lowered himself into a chair. When the fire was started, she turned around and demanded, "What are you sulking about anyway? I worked my ass all day and came home to no fire and no food. You wasted your time and got to come home to a fire, a meal, and a place to sleep. Isn't that right?"

Soapy remained silent, his expression neutral. "Isn't that right?" she repeated.

The boy lifted himself to his feet and noiselessly made his way to his room. To Chena, his silence demonstrated his ingratitude. Never so much as a word of thanks. It might be less galling if he were at least obedient. She realized that he would probably be entirely silent for the rest of the evening, and the thought angered her further. "Work or get worked!" she yelled, loudly enough for anyone who happened to be passing by to hear.

*

As she dished out the potatoes and rabbit, Chena called out to her son, "Food's ready, lazybones!"

Soapy ambled from his room, mechanically getting plates and a pitcher of water before joining his mother at the table.

The meal started as silently as Chena had expected but the boy was fidgety and agitated. After several minutes he spoke.

"When is Kilaun's brother leaving?" he huffed in an annoyed tone.

"Doesn't seem he is," she said. "Besides, what business is it of yours?"

"He ran his trap line near mine. I don't like it."

"Oh, your trap line, your trap line. That and girls is all you care about."

"You don't run your trap line alongside another man's!" he exclaimed. "Specially when that other man's been trapping that area for years, and 'specially when that other man is me!"

She challenged him, "What are you gonna do about it, Soapy? Fight him? He's three times your size."

"I might," he boasted with a whisper.

"If you do a stupid thing like that, you won't have a place to come home to even if you are lucky enough to survive! His brother keeps us housed and fed and you are not going to risk that over your damned fool trap line." She leaned across the table to make her point clear. Soapy didn't even look up. So obstinate. Useless. She had to put up with so much.

She grabbed his wrist firmly, "Ya hear me?"

He jerked his wrist away and stood up. "Yeah." He took his plate and left the table.

11

Qaniit found Chu on the porch, wrapped in blankets. She pulled her coat closed and sat down next to him on the bench. It was late morning, and the occasional townsperson meandered by in the middle of a chore or on their way to lunch. The mechanic walked by and smiled broadly. Qaniit quietly waved. Chu said nothing, and looked down.

"Is something bothering you?" she asked. What a fragile creature Chu was. Sensitive like a child. She figured her husband had been cruel to him. It made her angry.

He did not respond at first, and looked uncomfortable.

"Chu?"

Had he been crying? She leaned her head closer to look but he angled his face away when he detected the effort.

"Chu? Tell me what's wrong. Please tell me."

"The woman in the jail," he said simply.

Qaniit's heart broke for him.

"Is she not well?" she asked.

"No, not well. But she doesn't want me to cover the window."

Qaniit watched him. He fumbled with his hands.

"He needs to let her go. She's not so bad," Chu mumbled.

Qaniit admired Chu, in a way. He was so limited intellectually, and that had made his life more difficult than most, but his compassion and kindness remained intact throughout all of the suffering and cruelty he'd seen and endured. She would gladly have traded some of her husband's intellectual competence for some of Chu's empathy.

They spent some moments in silence. Seeing Chu suffer was hard for Qaniit. That he should be so selfless, blameless, and helpless all at the same time seemed terribly unfair.

"Will you speak at the assembly?" she asked, knowing the ridiculousness of her words even as she spoke.

"I don't…" He trailed off. "They would laugh."

"At you? Oh, no. No, they would never." Qaniit saw this fragile creature, worried, and wanted to comfort him. She sat closer, put her arm through his, and leaned her head against his arm.

The grumpy cook passed to the side of the house on the way to the root cellar. Qaniit saw her snort in disgust when she looked at them. Qaniit mused that to earn the disapproval of such a selfish and petty creature, she must be doing something right.

Qaniit stood up and said resolutely, "You are right that the woman has been in there for too long. I'll talk to Kilaun."

This appeared to give Chu some hope, but the sadness did not leave his eyes entirely. The man had endured much and demonstrated strong character. His sort of kindness and strength was something Qaniit felt the town needed more of.

*

"I went to see the prisoner," Qaniit told her husband.

His anger was explosive, which is what she had expected. As he rose to his feet, he demanded, "What business is it of yours?"

A man of his statute could win arguments simply by being physically imposing. If there had ever been a time when this kind of outburst would have cowed Qaniit, it was long past. She remained seated with poise as he hovered over her.

"It's my business because no one else has made it their business. She has done nothing wrong."

"You have no idea what she's done," he retorted.

"You're right, Kilaun, I don't. So tell me. What has this woman done to make her deserve to be locked in a dark, cold box, alone." Arguing with Kilaun was so rarely worth it that she'd almost abandoned the practice. But, now, Qaniit felt the indignation rising within her and it made her strong. Indignation for Chu as much as for the woman.

So it had been for everyone, she had to imagine. Dozens of people in the town, and they all just let this pass. Was it just as it had been with her? Perhaps disagreeing with Kilaun took too much effort, so they took the path of least resistance and let him have his way? What did that say about their community? And about Kilaun? And about Qaniit herself?

Kilaun stepped closer. She tried to look firm and resolute but felt as though she were physically shrinking under his gaze. Her eyes rose to meet his gaze but his unwavering intensity was too much. She looked away.

"Assembly in two days. You want to talk about that woman? We can do it there." He rumbled down the hallway.

The air felt different with Kilaun gone, as though the room itself had been holding its breath waiting for him to leave. And his rage and intensity had kept Qaniit at bay, in a sense. How had she not seen it when she'd married him?

No. He hadn't been this man when she'd married him. Perhaps she'd overlooked some flaws, but he hadn't been a tyrant.

Her confrontation had achieved nothing.

She went to sit in the great room. It was quiet, save for the sound of the women in the kitchen. She thought about the man her husband used to be. Driven to build something, not for his own sake, but for the sake of those that needed it. He built this town from nothing to something. There were no other towns that were doing as well as theirs.

Was he right? Was being so harsh and demanding the only way to keep people alive in this world?

Kilaun claimed he didn't want a government, but was that just because it allowed him to be the government? He had the power to put a woman in jail, indefinitely, and for little reason.

Qaniit wanted the woman let out. For a moment, she considered just walking over and freeing her. But the woman would have nowhere to go. In or out of a cell, the woman was going nowhere until spring. And nobody could come to get her until then, either.

Leif's cabin. It occurred to her in a flash. But she knew that Kilaun would look there if the woman were set free and couldn't be found in town, and that she'd be putting Leif at terrible risk. Given Kilaun's disdain for Leif, whose name he could barely speak, Qaniit could only imagine he would be grateful for the excuse to do something about him.

She considered how she might propose the woman's release at the assembly. While the woman's arrival had been a sensation, she had quickly disappeared as a topic of conversation. Now, it seemed as though she'd practically been forgotten. It...she...was a very inconvenient thing to talk about, or even to think about. Nobody had any reason to care about an outsider and, certainly, they had every reason to distrust her. And, of course, most importantly, everyone knew what Kilaun thought, and knew the consequences of thinking differently. Better to not think much at all than risk that.

Maybe it was time for thinking. Maybe it was time for talking. Maybe it had taken Chu to help her see the injustice, but Qaniit's eyes were not shut anymore. And, soon, her mouth would open as well. The result might be the same in the end, but at least this time not everyone would defer to Kilaun. Maybe by showing some courage herself, she would provide some to someone   else.

12

Leif was down the ladder, shoes on, gun in hand, and out the door before he realized he was awake. The cabin was dark and his eyes quickly adjusted. The moonlight reflecting off the snow made it seem bright as day. He fired a round into the ground, and ran over to the henhouse.

He saw a shadow run off into the trees, and blood on the ground outside the coop.

The only question was how bad it would be.

He could hear rustling in the back cages. That was good. Or bad, if it just meant he'd get to experience the death throes.

Goddamn wolves.

It wasn't the first time the wolves had come sniffing 'round his chickens that winter. He'd caught three in his traps. Too bad they weren't good for eating. At least he got some skins off of them.

He used the butt of his gun to put one hen out of her misery. The job had already been finished for him on another.

Shit.

Leif made sure the survivors were in the coop and laid out a few strategic traps around the small building. He dragged a heavy log across the yard and leaned it against the door. Those bastards wouldn't get any more of his hens tonight. But he wouldn't be getting back to sleep anytime soon either.

*

In the morning, Leif set to assessing the damage. He had found one already dead last night and been forced to kill another. Now, it looked as though a third was missing. Carried off, no doubt. The rooster was alive. He'd have to be careful with the eggs. He figured he would try to hatch a few inside during the winter, just to be safe.

He had a distant recollection of a time when he'd thought of wolves as noble. How funny, to have been that naïve. A life apart from nature afforded certain delusions. Since living in the cabin, Leif's delusions about wolves had been thoroughly dispelled.

By this point, he thought of them as automatic, visceral. When he looked at a wolf, he saw the cold, dead eyes of a predator. There was no sentimentality, no attempt to anthropomorphize the animals. They were his enemies. They knew it; he knew it.

Leif drank his spruce tea outside while he fixed up the henhouse. The loss of the chickens hurt, but the idea that those losses would help sustain the wolves added insult to injury. The bears never gave him this much trouble over the chickens. Although there weren't too many bears left in the area since the townspeople would kill them for meat. Leif was glad for that.

More bears than people, that's for sure. Don't hurt to have a few less of them and a few more of us.

He had picked through the snow by the front door, but couldn't find the shotgun slug. He hoped it would turn up in the spring. He didn't have so many shells left. Leif didn't know how to reload shells but he'd figure it out soon enough.

Someone in town probably knew how.

Until now, things had been quiet since Qaniit's visit. He'd thought about it often. Going so long between contact with one's fellow humans would do that. He had eaten the food she brought. The rhubarb was a nice change. He grew potatoes and cabbage himself, so that was more of the same, although a welcome more of course, but he hadn't grown rhubarb since his first season out. He wondered whether it was crazy to think of going to town to try to trade for a clump of the stuff to transplant. It was hardy stuff, from what he remembered.

He'd thought of other reasons to go to town. How had the dog healed up? Fine, of course, he knew that. Advice on melting down shells. Rhubarb. All fairly pitiful excuses.

The only excuse he didn't think of was the one reason he actually wanted to go – Taliriktug – his friend's daughter, now a young woman. A maid to Kilaun! Qaniit had said she was treated well, but Leif knew Kilaun did not treat anyone well.

She had been like a daughter to Leif those many years ago. Back when town was still open. Before Kilaun had become a tyrant. Before the people lived in fear.

But, of course, they had lived in fear, hadn't they? Fear of something different, though. Starvation, invasion, violence. Fear from without, not fear from within.

Kilaun was the one obstacle Leif's mind could not get past when he considered going to town. Leif wondered whether it was his own pride and anger he should blame for his loneliness, or the monster that Kilaun had become. There were times when Leif placed the blame squarely on himself. But he knew he simply could not coexist with the man.

How long will I survive alone like this?

With nobody to rely on? With nobody to talk to?

How long would I want to?

13

What a pathetic little coward!

Chena was sure that the maid girl was hiding in the root cellar. She stormed out of the kitchen and across the yard. She burst into the root cellar to find the girl inspecting jars of fruit. Chena pulled her out by her hair, the girl stifling her squeals and gasps of pain to the best of her ability. They argued in hushed voices on the way to the house.

"You shouldn't hide from him!" Chena snapped.

"I'm not – wasn't hiding," Tali stuttered.

"I'm not stupid. I know damn well what you were doing!"

"I just—" Tali's voice cracked.

"Don't even try to talk back to me. Everyone here treats you like you're something special. You're weak and you're stupid is what you are. Now get back in the house and do what needs doing before I have to smack you."

"But—" a sob burst forth from the girl.

When the promised slap arrived, the girl saw she couldn't win. She stumbled back inside, resigned to her fate.

"Oh, she's got it rough, hasn't she?" Chena thought sarcastically. *"Only good for one thing and she doesn't even want to do that. She's too lazy and stupid for anything else, so how the hell does she think she's supposed to survive?"*

Chena wished she were young enough to turn a man's head and get out of kitchen work. She figured that work done lying on one's back was better than work done breaking one's back. Besides, Chena wasn't going to cover for that girl every time Kilaun came 'round looking for her because he was mad at his wife.

*

When Chena followed after Tali, the girl was running a rag over a table, absentmindedly. Chena pushed by her, bumping into her as she passed. The girl was shaking.

"Watch out, some of us have actual work to do," Chena quipped as she left the kitchen with a thermos of hot water. She knew the girl hated her and didn't care. The girl was learning a lesson about power and survival. As for Chena, she was there to do her job. Anyone who made that job more difficult was not likely to draw a kind word from her.

Chena went into Kilaun's office and found him staring into space from his desk. She slammed the thermos on the desk, disrupting his thoughts.

"Hot water," she said.

"Good."

She turned to leave and paused with second thought. "Maid's back," she told him.

"Oh, good. Send her in."

Chena smiled, satisfied with herself.

14

Soapy checked his traps and found barely more than nothing. He was furious. He was sure it was because of Kilaun's brother laying his traps too close. The newcomer probably figured he could get away with anything since he was related to an asshole chief.

Soapy found one shitty little rabbit, half-dead in the trap.

Is he trying to put me in my place? He probably thinks I don't matter. I won't do anything. He's too big, he's Kilaun's brother and I'm nothing. Fuck him. I'd like to slit his fucking throat.

In a fit of rage, Soapy slammed the half-dead rabbit into a rock, killing it on impact. He didn't even bother to retrieve it.

The more Soapy thought about it, the angrier he became. He wanted to go to the assembly with something to offer. Maybe a lynx to eat, or at least a wolf for the dogs. What was he supposed to do with a half dead little hare?

This stuff with Kilaun's brother would have to stop. Soapy couldn't let it go on like this. He didn't care if his mother was angry with him. She would be angry with him no matter what he did. He made up his mind to confront Kilaun's brother, and force him to lay his traps elsewhere.

It was time to demand some respect. If he put a big guy like Chu in his place, nobody would fuck with him.

Soapy reset his traps and set to hiking back down the mountain.

*

Kilaun's brother was walking across town that afternoon when Soapy got back from trapping. Soapy started toward him, and the brother saw him coming.

"Hello," Chu said, happily. He was probably happy because he'd been eating Soapy's lynx meat.

"Listen, you," Soapy started, looking up, and pointing his finger at Chu's chest. He wanted to make it real clear to this guy that he meant business. "I don't 'preciate the way you been runnin' your traps."

The dimwit brother kind of cocked his head. As if he had no idea what Soapy was talking about.

"I'm telling you to run your traps somewhere else."

"Where?" he asked.

"I don't care!" Chu was emotionally non-responsive, so Soapy felt momentum on his side. Righteous anger spurred him on. "I been laying traps there for a decade," he exaggerated, "and you just show up and think you don't need to respect nobody. That ain't how it works. You find your own damned spot or I'll see it you got no teeth to eat with no how." By the end of his tirade, his finger was pointing at Chu just inches from the big man's face.

"Okay," Chu offered, looking disappointed and confused.

Soapy glared for a moment, then stamped past Chu, brushing against him on the way past.

Soapy replayed it in his mind over and over again. Respect isn't given, it's taken. And he'd taken it.

"See you at assembly tomorrow," Kilaun's brother called out as Soapy walked away. Chu's friendly tone of voice confirmed that Soapy had won, but it annoyed him all the same. He allowed himself a brief look back to admire the effect he'd had.

Soapy stomped the rest of the way through town to his mother's cabin feeling like a man to be reckoned with.

14.5

In Libby's more lucid moments, it occurred to her that she might not have long. She realized that things were getting worse. Between the cold and the hunger, she didn't have the energy to feel or care or want or hope. She did not want to die but she had come to terms with the probability. From daybreak to sunset, there was nothing to do but exist. There was a sense of boredom, but it was too faint to really be much of a bother.

With a detached interest, she wondered if she'd know if she were on the verge of death.

Libby would entertain herself at night by pressing her bare feet against the cold, dirt floor. She would start with the balls of her feet, moving up to her toes, until her foot was pressed completely down. The muscles in her feet would involuntarily tense from the coldness, but she would focus intently to overcome the urge. She would then wait. Soon enough, the floor would stop feeling cold. Instead, it felt like a force was emanating upwards, sucking the strength from her calves, making them seize up with cramps, stealing her body heat.

After ten minutes, the cramps became nearly unbearable, but in a strange sort of way, the exercise made Libby feel alive. It reminded her that she was human. If she could feel pain, then she would someday feel something other than pain. Pain was better than feeling nothing, and it was a hell of a lot better than feeling helpless. Feeling the strength leaving her reminded her that she had some strength left. So Libby made that her ritual and, every night, she opened herself up to feeling human again.

15

Kilaun's breathing changed. He'd fallen asleep. Tali got dressed quickly and silently and left without a word.

She hated the things she had to do with him. She wished she knew how to stop it, but it was too late now that it had started. That was partly her fault. The first time he pressed against her, she had frozen. Maybe if she had tried to move away or something, but she didn't. She never told him to stop or said no. She should have known better than to be alone in a room with a man anyhow, but she never thought of Kilaun as a man who would be weak in that way. It had never occurred to her that a man married to someone like Qaniit could want Tali in that way.

Now, every time she thought of Qaniit, Tali felt a flash of guilt. Qaniit was one of the few people who treated Tali like a human being, and Tali had betrayed her. How proud Tali had been to count her as a friend. Sometimes, she could pretend it wasn't happening. Then, the shame and the fear would stay hidden and life could feel normal for a while.

She emerged from the hall into the kitchen, which was devoid of people and in need of cleaning. Good. She didn't have to worry about Kilaun calling for her again for the rest of the day, and cleaning could keep her busy so she wouldn't have to think about what had just happened.

As long as Chena stayed away, that is. That knowing smirk of hers; she seemed to enjoy shaming Tali. Tali hated her more than she hated Kilaun. Men were always doing awful things for sex, but Chena was cruel and horrible just because she could be – hitting her and calling her worthless, mainly. It had only intensified since things with Kilaun had begun.

Her father would have protected her. Kilaun would not have done it if Tali's father were still alive. Her father had taken care of her, and she of him.

Upon closer inspection, the kitchen was in worse shape than she had realized. The counter was filthy, covered in dishes from cooking. Tali got started. She had always cleaned when something was bothering her, even before becoming a maid. Now, with so many troubles, she worked feverishly.

This thing with Kilaun had been going on for three months.

That first time, before she realized how it was going to be, it was kind of nice having his attention. She had tried in vain to forget that she'd felt that way at first. But, horrible though he was, he was strong and handsome, and to capture the attention of someone so powerful made Tali feel interesting and important and…grown-up.

The second time she just felt disloyal. And used. And dirty. She scrubbed the countertops with renewed vigor.

Tali had been spending more and more time lost in thought about how she might get away from Kilaun. She hoped he'd just forget about it, but would he forget about it before she got pregnant? With her luck, probably not.

There was nowhere for Tali to go, and no other job for her to take. A few women were envious that she got the job as a maid in the main house. She did not have to haul or chop or grovel, so much as they knew. They'd probably be jealous if they knew she was sleeping with Kilaun. She had heard them giggling and whispering about what he would be like in bed. Only because they didn't know him, though.

Sometimes she wished Qaniit would find out. She wondered if it would be worth Qaniit hating her to get away from Kilaun. She was sure that Qaniit would not allow it to continue. But then Tali might have to leave. A friend of hers had gotten mixed up with one of the married men and was sent away before anyone knew she was pregnant. Lord only knew to where, probably the Pass, or even down to the Port.

If Tali could be sure she'd get sent to the Pass and not the Port, she probably would have risked it. She either would have run away herself or told Qaniit and got sent away. The Pass was a four-day trek up the river, which was ice this time of year. Chu had come down after the river froze, but that's too hard a trip for most people. Sure, it's quicker than in summer, but you're also quicker to freeze to death or break an ankle or get stranded without food. Tali figured her best bet was in the spring. If she went to the Pass, that's when she'd go.

There were only a few families left out at the Pass, and Chu had said they weren't doing well. The word was that there wasn't enough food, but sometimes Kilaun talked after he was done, and he said the real problem was lack of organization. People looking out for themselves and not the community, no use of specialties. Each family might as well have been off on their own without the town at all, because everyone did everything for themselves. Kilaun said that this was inefficient, and that a town could never grow if they kept operating that way, and lacking good fortune, they'd continue to starve and die off.

Tali thought maybe she could help them with organization. She knew about running a town. Her father had talked to her about those things all the time. He might not have been head of the town like Kilaun, but he was smart man, and could have been head if he had wanted to. He knew a lot about government. He said it was because of what he knew that he didn't want to have anything to do with it.

So, if Tali got pregnant or just couldn't take it anymore, she could always go to the Pass. Chu said there were cabins there that no one was living in. She knew it'd be hard, but no harder than life now. Tali knew how to trap, cook, and keep healthy. That might be enough. Eventually, order would be reestablished and she could hold out until then. Maybe even eventually move to a city Outside. Yet, she didn't know about those things so she tried not to think too much about them.

The other option was the Port. That's where she'd get sent if things went poorly. It sounded like hell. Full of angry, lonely men, preying on sad, hungry women. The men fished and the women sold themselves. And whenever a government from the Outside sent someone up, they came through the Port. Twice new governments had sent up military expeditions and swept the town clean of resources. The people just started over again, fishing and whoring. No, thank you, Tali would stay here as whore to Kilaun before she whored to an entire village of ruffians.

She got the kitchen as clean as it could get, and just in time, too. Chena charged in yelling about something or other. For the next two days, they would be focusing on getting ready for the assembly, which would require a good deal of food preparation.

They'd be busy. That was good.

16

Soapy was getting water from the spring when his mother came down to get him. She stood glaring silently for a moment, arms akimbo, before delivering her news.

"Kilaun wants to see you." She spat the words out as though they tasted like rancid meat.

He didn't bother to either acknowledge that he'd heard her or comment on the judgment in her face. His mother was the least of his worries for the moment. He put the lids on his buckets and turned back toward his house. He set them by the back door and headed for Kilaun's.

Chu. This had to be about Chu. What had Chu told Kilaun? Probably lies.

He tried to think of any alternative to this being a consequence of his provocation of Kilaun's idiot brother, but came up with nothing. Hungry just moments before, he now felt sick to his stomach with worry. Kilaun yelling was unpleasant enough but, if it became physical, Kilaun would pulverize him, and who knew given his rages when he'd stop. Or worse, Soapy could be thrown in a cell. He wished he'd stopped and gotten an extra sweater from the house.

Soapy found his apprehension had led him to quicken his pace. Getting there quickly seemed like a bad idea. He needed to think. He was in the right regarding the dispute with Chu. Kilaun was a man, he could understand. Soapy figured that framing his explanation in terms of how Chu's trapping strategies were hurting the village resources was his best strategy.

The only other times he'd been at the house, he'd been there with his mother. Soapy went in through the kitchen out of habit. It was easily the nicest house he'd ever seen, always clean and warm, with plenty of lights.

The maid was there in the kitchen when he walked in. They briefly made eye contact but she immediately looked down. He'd love to get that one out of her clothes, but so would every other man in town. The way his mother talked, a lot of them must have. His mother was always around when he tried talking to the maid and she'd inevitably butt in or find something else the girl should be doing.

No mother this time. But Soapy was in no mood to even make the attempt, and the girl looked no more receptive than usual anyhow. So he just tipped his hat and went on through to the main room.

He didn't know whether he should look for Kilaun or sit and wait. Before he had the chance to reach a decision, Kilaun burst in. "I need to talk to you, young man."

Soapy thought it an odd choice of words given that he was nearly 40, and he wondered whether it was because of his small stature. He tried to sit up a little straighter.

"I have a business proposition for you."

"You've come to the right man," Soapy said without pause. He tried not to emphasize the word 'man,' but then he thought he might have anyway. He was thoroughly relieved to know this wasn't about Chu and the traps. He stood up to join Kilaun, and walked down a hallway to the chief's private office.

Soapy had never been in this room before. It was tiny, a closet really, but well appointed. It had a shiny desk, and maps, and pens, and all the things a gentleman would need to command a village. Kilaun was more stylish than Soapy had realized.

"Have a seat… Soapy, right?"

"Yes, Sir." Now Soapy sounded like a kid, but he couldn't help it. He sat in wonder, looking at all the trinkets and devices in the nooks and crannies of the office. The chair was sturdy and comfortable, but a little oversized.

"Would you like to smoke?" Kilaun asked, as he took out a pouch from his desk.

Soapy quickly nodded. He missed smoking.

Kilaun rolled a cigarette and passed the pouch to Soapy. Kilaun lit his cigarette, and started talking as Soapy rolled his own.

"I would like to get my wife a present."

Soapy looked up and nodded before going back to his rolling.

"A horse, actually. I'd like her to have a horse to ride."

Soapy was finished rolling, and wanted to light his cigarette, but the matches were across the desk. Kilaun looked deep in thought, so he didn't interrupt yet.

"Of course, the problem is there are no horses."

"No, we don't have any round here. Maybe down at the Port."

"I sent someone down to ask at the Port. They ate whatever horses they had."

Soapy stared at the matches across the desk, dying to light his cigarette. Kilaun sat across from him, puffing away. Kilaun stood up and looked out the window, oblivious to Soapy's desperation.

"There was a man, though, a few years back, living up near the glacier toe."

"Oh, Leif," Soapy said, starting to reach across the desk.

"Do you know him?" Kilaun asked excited, spinning around.

Soapy snapped his hand back, startled. "Very limited dealings, Sir, years ago."

"Well, from what I hear, he had horses, at least as of a couple years ago," Kilaun said.

"I believe he did, Sir."

"I want you to go out to this man's cabin, and if he has a horse, I want you to trade him for it."

"Trade him what?" The matches felt so very far away.

"Food, skins, ammo even."

Soapy leaned back, sure he would never get to smoke. "What if he doesn't want to sell?"

Kilaun turned around and looked at him. "Come here," he beckoned Soapy to come to the window. Soapy set his cigarette on the desk and complied.

Kilaun put his hand on Soapy's shoulder and looked him square in the eyes. "I'm hiring you to bring me a horse. I don't particularly care whether the man is happy about it or not." He pointed in the direction of the glacier toe. "That man contributes *nothing* to this community. If all he has to do is sell a horse after half a dozen years of living here, hunting the woods we hunt, trapping the animals we trap, well that's still a minor contribution in my mind."

This Kilaun was smart. He didn't ask Soapy to steal the horse, but Soapy heard him loud and clear. Kilaun must have found out that Soapy was the kind of man who could get things done, breaking through traditional limitations and making things happen. This was just the kind of partnership Soapy was looking for.

Soapy nodded.

"Don't you want to know what I'll pay you?" Kilaun mused.

"Oh, I'm sure it'll be fair. I'll do it," Soapy said.

Kilaun raised his eyebrows, as if to say, "Of course you will." But he said nothing. He put his hand on Soapy's back to lead him out of the room. Soapy desperately wanted to go back across the office and fetch his cigarette, but he didn't get the impression he was welcome to do so.

Kilaun let Soapy show himself out, and Soapy restrained himself by not stealing anything on his way through the house. He passed through the kitchen hoping to see the maid but only his angry mother was in there with a sour look on her face.

That night, Soapy dreamt about all the tobacco that Kilaun would give him if he brought back a horse.

17

In the morning, Kilaun woke with a sickness in his stomach. It was the day for assembly, and he still did not know how to solve the problem of the Minarchist. It was particularly cold the night before and if he had her dragged out to the assembly she'd probably cough and carry on a show. He still didn't want to kill her and he didn't want to let her go. There were no good options.

Kilaun looked to the other side of the bed and found it empty. Nor was his wife on the couch across the room where she had taken to sleeping. She would pretend like she fell asleep there while drawing, but he was sure she was doing it on purpose. One more insult to endure from his wife.

He hoped the horse would win her back. He had no other ideas. He had accepted long ago that she was beyond his understanding. His love for her was his curse.

He pulled back the covers and frigidness greeted him. He quickly dressed and went down to the kitchen. The cook and the maid were preparing food for the assembly.

"What is there to eat?" he asked.

The maid wouldn't make eye contact. He didn't have time for her sort of teasing this morning.

The cook answered, "There's some bear on the counter there," her arms were full of vegetables so she gestured with her head. "Tali! Get him a plate."

"No, I don't care," Kilaun said. He pulled the knife off his belt and lopped off a chunk. It was fatty and warm. He left the kitchen tearing a bite off, grease dripping down the side of his hand and arm.

It tasted like the shoulder off a young black. Probably that one the lumberman killed last fall. The glacier bear had wandered over from lord only knew where. The bear had been stalking the lumberman from the edge of the yard, which was aggressive behavior. There had been only one other glacier bear out this way in the last six years, and it had met a similar fate, but for hunger, not aggression.

The lumberman did not have any ammo and had come to Kilaun to get some. He made a fair trade, just some of the meat for the shells. Early the next morning, while still in bed, Kilaun heard a shot ring out announcing that the lumberman would have a busy morning of cleaning ahead of him.

Kilaun envied him for that. Something about gutting a big animal was very appealing to him. He thought about the joy of getting up to his elbows in blood, and regretted only that on that particular morning, he had other commitments so could not help the lumberman. Nonetheless, he was glad for the trade, as this particular piece of meat made losing a couple shells well worth it.

He chewed the last bite while staring out the window of the great room. The occasional townsperson walked by, doing their chores of hauling water or deadwood, or fetching a coal from the neighbors due to a lost fire. Kilaun wondered if any of them realized how much work was required to build and maintain the framework in which they could comfortably live their lives.

He figured they had no idea, but knew it was his charge to care for them anyway. He was the agent of the ancestors and they had stationed him here in this pitiful little town. Until they gave him the assignment of going elsewhere, he would manage this place to the best of his ability. That included preparing a strategy for the assembly that would take place that night.

Kilaun headed to his office to do exactly that.

18

Chu decided that it was definitely getting colder as he lumbered to the shed.

He looked among the tools and picked out a hammer, some nails, and a scrap of wood. He saw some old paints and grabbed those too.

He took the paints inside and found Tali in the kitchen. She gave him a shy smile and said hello.

"What's all that stuff?" she asked, bustling around.

When he didn't respond, she took several steps in his direction to see for herself.

Chu jerked to hide them, but then opened his hand and let her see. "They're frozen."

She pulled a pot off the stove. "You can put them here to heat them up if you'd like." She gestured to the floor under the stove. "I could make you some tea while you waited."

This prompted a grateful smile from Chu, though it fell short of his usual giant grin. He seated himself in the only chair in the room. He realized that he couldn't feel his toes so a few extra moments in the warm kitchen were welcome. He put the hammer and wood down and let himself warm up.

"What can I paint with, Tali? I didn't see any brushes."

She thought and he waited. "How about…" She leaned and whispered, "A tiny cut off Kilaun's coat?"

Chu gasped and the girl giggled. But he thought she was right, hair would be fine. He could wrap it on a twig with some string. Or a porcupine quill! "Any there quills around here?"

She frowned. "Early this winter, I got a few out of Gun before… Well, take a look out back on top of the barrel and they might still be there, never know." She handed him some tea and went back to work.

After his toes were warmed up, Chu went out back and saw the barrel covered in snow. He knocked the top layer off and picked through what was left. Some washers, nails, and, there they were, several quills.

He went back in and found the kitchen empty. He grabbed his tools and thawed paints and headed out to the porch.

Chu set the piece of wood on his lap, got his paints ready and his quill, and looked at the trees for inspiration. There were no leaves on the aspens, but he knew what they looked like when there were. So he set to painting the aspens with their trembling leaves, with the summer sky and clouds behind them.

*

It wasn't a prison really. They called it a prison, but only because the people that stayed there were prisoners. It was actually a basement in an old mill. There were three rooms, two of which were "cells," and all of which had dirt floors and little else. Someone had put bars in the narrow windows after an industrious prisoner managed to work himself free. But the bars were just fire-treated spruce poles and Chu figured he could probably break one if he really wanted to.

The woman from Outside had been the only one there for some time. Chu went to her cell and knocked on the door.

She did not answer.

He put the things he was carrying down and opened the door. She was lying in the bed, curled up facing the wall. He couldn't see her face.

"Miss?" he asked.

"My name's Libby," she answered. Her voice was hoarse. She coughed a little. She didn't sound mad, though.

Chu just stood there, not sure what to do. "Do what you came for," the woman said, without turning to look at him. Chu shrugged. The way she looked now confirmed that he really did have to close up the window. He would arrange a lantern for her if he could, although he hoped she would be released after assembly tonight.

He went to the window and started putting up the wood. "Assembly is tonight. Did you know?"

"What's that?"

"My brother called assembly to talk about you," he said.

"Your brother?" she asked, still facing away from him.

"Kilaun. The leader." Chu had finished nailing up the first side.

She snorted, then started coughing again. He understood she was angry. She was entitled to be, he thought. His brother was not being honorable about this. Chu couldn't remember how long the woman had been there, but he thought it was since he got to town, which seemed like a while ago.

Chu finished nailing up the second side of the board. There was a little light coming in from between the logs near the top, so at least it wasn't completely dark.

"Well, I hope Kilaun lets you go," he said. "You don't sound good."

And with that, he left, hammer in hand, locking up behind him.

19

Nearly all winter days were the same for Leif. Depending upon his mood, this could be either a comfort or an irritant.

Inevitably, he'd awaken before dawn. The days were so short and the nights so long that it couldn't be helped. A trip outside to empty his bladder and bowels provided an opportunity to check on the chickens and horses as well, and he'd return to the cabin with the kindling and logs he needed for a fire.

The hour or more spent tending the fire while drinking tea was often the most enjoyable part of his day. It was time that couldn't be spent doing the harder labor outside, so he was able to sit peacefully drinking tea if he chose. At other times, he'd read, or clean, and if there were eggs he'd eat.

At mid morning when the sun came up, Leif went outside and did his chores. He would gather kindling and put it in the woodshed to dry if the pile was getting low. He would cut some deadwood to use in the stove. He would haul water from the nearby spring, and one of his horses would drag it the half mile to his house on a sled. If something needed fixing, he'd fix it. He would feed the animals and exercise the horses. Especially when the days were at their shortest, there was very little daylight left over.

When Leif first started living this far north, that was the big drawback to having so little light – the race to get his chores done. Now he did his chores as quickly as necessary, and was ready to go in by the time the light petered out. Soon enough, the cold would drive him inside before the darkness did.

Having so little light forced Leif to build a routine and stick to it. He had tried it the other way in early years – waking up whenever he did (which would be when the sun came up, late), cutting wood as he needed it. But he came to understand that he was happiest with a routine, and that it was less stressful to pile up on wood and let it dry out well before trying to use it. He believed that taking care of himself in the little ways was what had allowed him to survive and stay sane in a cold, dark and unwelcoming climate.

When he was done with his chores, he went inside and tried to thaw out. He put some wood in the box and soup on the stove. He read by lamplight, or puttered about the house and fixed things. More than anything else, he simply thought. More and more, it seemed like all he could think of was the past. Reliving it. It was not an altogether pleasant pastime, but he seemed less able to help himself than ever.

Before Leif went to bed each night he would go out to check on the horses. He would set a small fire in the stable stove if it were particularly cold in there. Sometimes he would talk to the horses for a while. For the first few years, he remained convinced that the conversations were for the horses' benefit, but by this point he'd admitted they were for him. He needed to hear language.

To feel human, perhaps, or to remind himself he was capable of it.

The horses were indifferent.

Leif usually laid down to sleep before he was tired. He would lay and stare at his patchwork ceiling in the firelight. He would review his day and think about the next one, what he had done and what still needed doing.

After he was done with that, everything would become quiet. He could hear perfectly the crackle of the fire, the sliding of snow off the roof, even the voles making tunnels in the snow and under his cabin. He owned these moments, moments of freedom, moments without obligation. He was surrounded by a life of his making, and each sound was a precious thing, belonging only to him. It was at these times when he felt his life was rich, when he felt both the most alone and the least lonely. Savoring his hard earned moments of peace, Leif would gradually drift off to sleep, resting his old body for a night just like the one before it.

20

Libby continued dozing after the big man left. She felt some curiosity regarding the assembly and the potential of something other than just existing under a huddled mass of blankets, but it wasn't enough to keep her awake.

It also registered as odd that this enormous man, seemingly so kind, could be the brother of that other man, who she'd hate if she could muster the energy.

In the moments of semi-consciousness, she wondered about this assembly and whether she would be brought to attend. In the old days, a person got to defend herself when she was accused of wrongdoing. At the very least, she got to know what she were accused of. Libby knew she'd done nothing wrong and she also knew that offered no protection. Being "other" had been punishable by death for all of human history. She shuddered at the thought. It already felt like she was dead, so being dead wasn't frightening. But death, having to actually die, that still made her feel fearful.

But at least it was feeling something. It wasn't entirely unpleasant.

It was darker than before. Libby knew the big man had boarded up the window. She had heard him crashing about, but was too exhausted to look and see what he was doing. She knew it was probably for the better. It had been way too cold.

She rolled over onto her back and opened her eyes. A lone ray of light shined from a hole in the floor above and across the room onto the wood panel that covered the window. She found herself marveling at the beauty she saw.

Thin, fragile trees, reaching toward the sky. Small, delicate leaves on every branch. The sun dancing on each leaf. She could feel life in the trees and they felt more alive than she remembered ever feeling. Alive and free and beautiful, standing proudly in their own world that contained nothing but themselves and a crisp blue sky.

A painting. She couldn't think of why. Why he'd done this for her.

Was it an accident? The only thing he could spare to cover the window?

No. This wasn't something anyone would throw away, was it? He knew she loved the view out the window. Was this his apology for covering it? She felt moved by the gesture. And then moved by the knowledge that something had penetrated her frozen, malnourished carcass, that it had been proven to her that she was still alive.

And wanted to stay that way.

Libby watched the painted trees the same way she would have watched the sky before the barrier became necessary. Except now there was no breeze. And there was a spark within her.

21

"I can handle things long enough for you to go change," the cook snapped at the maid. "You look a mess."

Tali inadvertently sighed audibly while removing her apron, drawing a nasty glare from Chena.

Chena was stressed with assembly coming on. The food was cooked and ready to set out but Tali was still in her maid's clothes. Chena wasn't as worried about her own appearance. She wasn't the kind to go announcing her opinions on everything in front of the whole town anyway, so no one would probably even look at her. And the girl had finding a husband to think about. Chena was too old for that nonsense.

That little girl Sila was helping again. Well, she was less help than trouble, but Qaniit had her sent in. She was inspecting the dishware to make sure it was clean. So long as she wasn't under Chena's feet, Chena didn't care what the girl did.

She checked the set up in the great room. Chairs and stools set around the room, some crates, a few cuts of spruce trunk turned on end – anywhere someone could put their butt. She counted under her breath and figured on 22 people plus Kilaun. The mechanic's wife was sick with pregnancy, and couldn't leave the house. So he'd probably leave the young boy home as well to tend to her.

Not that it mattered exactly how many would be there. The dining table only sat 8 at most. So Chena would put out food enough for all and people could help themselves.

Kilaun would not eat with them. Chena chuckled to herself. He was always acting so serious-minded, but come assembly he got stage fright like a little boy.

The room was warm enough, and it would probably become too warm once they got the hot breath of 23 people in there. She made sure there was extra wood by the firebox just in case. She put a large pot of water on and dropped in her own special blend of spruce tea. It was cold enough outside that even a short walk would leave their guests desperately cold, plus Chena was proud of her secret recipe.

She went back in the kitchen and found Sila dragging a piece of wood over to the open stove. "No!" she barked.

It alarmed the little girl, who dropped the wood and cowered. "It was getting cold, I thought-"

"No, you didn't think." Chena pushed the girl out of the way and closed the stove. "We don't need any more heat with all the people we got coming in here." That girl was more trouble that she was worth. "Go sweep," and Chena gestured to the great room. It'd already been swept, but it'd get the girl out of the kitchen.

The girl shuffled off, leaving Chena to focus on getting the food in dishes. She had just finished scooping the vegetables into a big wooden bowl when Kilaun's idiot brother rumbled in the back door looking agitated.

She turned to him and put her hand on her hip. "Yes?"

He'd seemingly been stammering since before he knew she was there but she was able to make out that he wanted to know if she'd seen Kilaun.

"Yes, I've seen him." And she turned around as if that ended the matter. When she didn't hear him leaving she turned around and added, "He's busy and so am I, so get moving!"

"But I need to talk to him!" the imbecile blurted out. She could not believe he would raise his voice at her, and she did not intend to tolerate it. Sila got no farther than barely in the room before Chena took the broom from her and chased Chu outside with it. "Don't come back till assembly!" she huffed, slamming the door closed.

She spent the next twenty minutes working up a sweat, getting the food in dishes and out onto the table in the great room. Naturally, that Tali was nowhere to be found. "Only useful on her back anyhow, that one," Chena thought disdainfully.

She had just gotten everything set up when there was a knock on the door and the first of the townspeople arrived. Chena went to the door and found the lumberman, his wife, and their infant. She pursed her lips, thinking about how annoying it'd be if that baby took to crying. Selfishly forcing their baby on everyone else, of course. They probably expected her to coo over it the way a lot of the women in town seemed to. She scowled instead.

The lumberman and his wife took their outside gear off and piled it in the hallway. There'd be a mighty big pile by the time all the townspeople got in there and undressed. Boots, scarves, hats, coats, mitts. The ones that came from farther off might have winter pants as well. Chena took their gear and hauled it back to Kilaun's office.

She opened the door and found Kilaun sitting at his desk. He looked at her without moving. Chena piled the coats in the chair across from him. She put her hand on her hip.

"You want a plate of food?" she asked.

"No."

"I can have the maid bring it," she offered, a hint of flirtation in her voice.

"I'm fine." The gruff tone in his response indicated that the discussion was now over. He was doing his big important man act. Fair enough.

When she got back out to the great room, a few more townspeople had arrived, and they were sitting around the room, greeting one another and chatting. Sila had given up on helping and cooed in front of Soapy, who had just come in and finished getting his coat off.

"Well, go on and eat!" Chena commanded to the room of visitors.

Soapy hustled across the room but she smacked his stomach. "Don't be rude!"

He retreated, and the lumberman went first, lopping a hunk of smoked moose onto his plate.

Chena went back in the kitchen to get the last of the food and found the maid coming in the back door looking much more presentable than she did before.

"Bout time," Chena snorted.

"Sorry," Tali mumbled. She was a pretty girl, but Chena didn't understand why Kilaun and Soapy were both so fond of her. She was too spineless, no strength of will. Just a pretty face, really, and everyone knows those don't last. Tali took her coat off and Chena saw she was wearing a dress. Soapy would be falling all over himself tonight to sit by her. He was such an embarrassment.

After surveying the kitchen to see that everything was taken care of, Chena took her apron off, smoothed down her hair, and went out to join the guests.

22

As Qaniit crouched down behind the barrel, she heard the rhythmic crunching of paws in the snow coming toward her. From the darkness emerged the dog called Gun. He trotted up to her and gave her a lick on the face.

"All right, all right," she said soothingly. He calmed and sat next to her. She gave him a good rubbing before reaching into her coat pocket and pulling out her husband's leather tobacco pouch. She knew at this very moment he was probably reaching for it in his desk, cursing to find it gone, and she relished the idea. She noticed herself getting more daring in teasing Kilaun in the last two months. Getting to know Chu, seeing how he dismissed his brother, sharing his perspective – it had made her braver.

She rolled a cigarette and used a match to light it. Gun sat and panted, watching the sky with her, occasionally scratching behind his ear. Her left arm hung loosely around him and her right lifted the cigarette to her mouth.

It was well into December and the frozen world was gorgeous. A good two feet of snow on the ground, and icicles hung over her from the eaves on the house. Past the icicles, she could see the sky, crystal clear with the brightest stars. The archer was not out yet, but she tried to calculate where he was from the other stars. Just over the eastern horizon, she thought.

The trees were majestic. The aspens stood tall and naked, ice coating every cranny of their ornate branches. Their tiny branch clusters looked like giant snowflakes. Qaniit subtly moved her head to watch the starlight pass behind the ice.

In the background, Qaniit could hear the chatter of the rest of the town inside eating. She knew she should make her way inside, as her absence would be noticed, but the selfish pleasure of the cigarette and the beauty surrounding her was too much to leave just then. It felt like she'd escaped and gone into hiding, especially with the constant reminder of the crowd inside provided by the sound of movement and talk she could just make out. It had been a long time since she felt like she could come and go as she pleased.

But it was too good to last, of course. Her solitude was broken when she heard the approach of footsteps. She was still crouched behind the barrel, so someone coming from the side of the house would not see her. She leaned forward to peek around the barrel and saw Chu, staring at her sky.

"Chu?" she whispered.

"Qaniit?" he peered into the darkness. She caught his eye.

"What are you doing back there?" Gun ran over to him as he approached. They greeted one another.

"Indulging a bit," she responded, and held up the end of the cigarette. "You want any?"

He shook his head no. "You okay?" he asked.

She took her last drag and dropped the cigarette in the snow. It fizzled. She stood up and shook her legs awake, brushing the snow off the front of her pants. "Oh, I'm fine. You okay?"

"I was just looking for you," he said. "I can talk to my brother about the prisoner."

"You sure?" she asked, even though he sounded resolute.

"Yes. He is my brother." It was clear that Chu viewed this as unassailable logic, though it obviously hadn't occurred to him until recently.

She shook her head and understood. Chu was a simple man, but noble. He did not fear his brother; he only craved his affection. She had once craved her husband's kindness as much as Chu did, but the perpetual disappointment had led her to conclude it was a lost cause.

Chu stood there, with his jaw set, and he looked stronger than his brother. Qaniit admired him for his willingness to take on Kilaun.

She did not know what would happen if Chu challenged him at assembly. The treatment of the prisoner had not been acceptable. The townspeople had left too much to Kilaun in recent years. They had become lazy. Maybe it took someone like Chu who hadn't let his values slowly slip away to remind them of what they'd once wanted for themselves. Maybe people would finally stand up.

"You are such a good man, Chu," Qaniit told him. She realized she felt like a mother talking to her son. But she had not had a son for a long time and that thought stabbed at her psyche for a moment before she was able to expel it.

Chu reached toward her and placed his hand firmly on her neck, behind her ear and under her hair. He looked at her and responded, simply, "Thank you."

Chu took his hand back and went inside. Qaniit stood outside, her body now tingling, wondering what had just happened.

23

Kilaun made no perceptible effort to attract attention, but the atmosphere changed immediately upon his entering the room. Not only did the idle chatter natural in such a crowd cease, but all the townsfolk seemingly fell motionless. Not a sound, not a movement, but for Kilaun's long strides gracefully moving him through the crowd.

Tali blushed and averted her eyes. In moments alone, she wanted nothing more than to get away from him, but seeing him like this always moved something inside her. She'd found a perverse pride at his desire for her since she'd become his...her mind allowed her no further. No good could come of defining their relationship.

He took his seat next to Qaniit in an old wooden chair upholstered in leather. It was no throne, but it was the nicest chair in town. When Kilaun looked at the townspeople, he looked at them with a love that he never shared with people as individuals.

"How is the winter?" he asked the room.

He was greeted only by an awkward silence for a few moments, but a brave soul finally spoke up, sparing the room further embarrassment by claiming the winter was treating them kindly. Empty plates were heaped on a tray on the dining table. The dishes of food had been picked clean, and the people had looks of fullness on their faces and in the way they moved. It wasn't often that Kilaun opened his home to everyone but, when he did, he was quite generous. The moose and salmon he put out could have fed his own household for a month.

The people settled in. Tali sat on a crate in the back of the room. The cook's son sat next to her and he let his leg fall at an odd angle until it pressed up against hers. She jerked her knee away. Why were they like this? She focused her attention on Kilaun.

The room grew quiet. The people watched him. The lumberman's wife hushed her baby. The mechanic forced himself to stifle the fidgeting of his legs. Qaniit, so tiny next to her husband, was the only one not watching Kilaun. Her gaze pointed downward toward her lap, where her hands were clasping one another. The townspeople waited patiently for Kilaun to speak.

"I am not your leader," Kilaun opened. There had been a time when this statement would've resulted in sideways glances amongst the townspeople. They were used to this sort of statement from him now, the words no longer meaning anything. It may just as well have been a greeting. The faces, ears, eyes, all moved imperceptibly closer, ready to hear what he had to say.

"I called you here because there is an important decision *you* must make," he continued, his face serenely calm. Each member of the audience felt Kilaun was speaking to him or her, the effect even more pronounced in those who'd barely ever spoken to the man.

His silences spoke as loudly as his words. He looked from person to person, strengthening his hold on his audience, letting the pauses augment the force of his breath.

"As you know, there is an Outsider staying in the basement of the old mill. The newest government on the mainland sent her. This time it's a 'Minarchy.' This woman, the Minarchist, says she was sent to establish contact, potentially a trade agreement, even an alliance."

Although most of this was already common knowledge, the people listened patiently.

"As your fellow citizen, as your friend, I could not help but be reminded of what happened at the Port when the last government decided to extend such an offer. I know that many of you had similar thoughts."

Some of the people shook their heads affirmatively. Tali saw eyes widening, and the collective pulse of the room quickened.

Three years ago, the Port had been destroyed by Outsiders seeking resources that the town simply didn't have to give them. Some survived, but only the coldest, fiercest people stayed there in town. Tali reckoned they must be armed to the teeth by now.

"I don't want to pay that same price here. I don't want to see the people I love butchered, the women of our town raped, our houses burned. But perhaps I am selfish to focus on those things. For myself, I find that my life is good, and I do not need whatever the Outsider thinks her masters have to offer me. Perhaps there are others here who feel differently."

There was quiet. This pause was ostensibly for others to interject, but everyone just waited for Kilaun to continue.

"Perhaps some of you are going hungry, and I do not know it? Or perhaps you fear for your safety here? Please, if so, now is the time to say something."

Not so much as an audible breath emerged from any mouth but Kilaun's.

"I am glad. I am glad that you, my brothers and sisters, are safe and secure here with me. We have come a long way, built ourselves into something strong, together. And I think this Outsider, with her promises, can only bring us suffering. She cannot make things better for us. And with invasion, pillage, rape and murder being the possible price for any alliance this 'Minarchy' might propose, I cannot see how anything could be worth the risk.

"But you, my friends, speak, do you disagree?"

Several audible utterances of "no" were heard. Heads shook. His audience was with him.

Kilaun lifted his chin. "I know you, and I know you do not want to see this place destroyed. Each of you loves this town as much as I, and each have invested a great deal into its success. And we are successful, thanks to each of you!" His showed the room his clenched fist.

Some of the men sat up straighter at the thought, suddenly struck by pride. Kilaun looked them in the eyes, even the old butcher, who was similarly stirred into dignity by the praise despite his near blindness and usual confusion.

"This woman, she came representing the government that will kill and destroy each of you and your families, if given the chance."

Grumbles of agreement, of acknowledgement, moved about the room.

Tali felt uncomfortable. She felt they were all wrong, that they didn't know it. She wasn't used to believing she knew more than those around her. She'd been around the woman, just incidentally, feeding and caring for her. She was just a woman, weakened by cold, hunger, and loneliness. Tali wished she could make everyone understand that but simply had no idea how to go about it.

"So what are we to do with her? Do we let her go back to her people? Wouldn't she just tell her government where we are? I don't want to join the roster of damned towns in this territory."

Kilaun was a natural, varying his tone, his pace, his gaze and his motion, all tools to maximize the impact of his words, helping his audience identify with him and his point of view. As he built up to his climax, his gesticulations became more controlled, tighter, more assured.

"Well, we must decide tonight. Decide what to do with her. Should she be set free?"

Tali felt sick. The entire room was putty in his hands. They shook their heads firmly, some crying "No!" Everyone except Chu and Qaniit, who Tali saw glance quietly at one another.

Qaniit nodded to Chu, who spoke up, "Brother?"

Kilaun said, "Friends, this is my brother, who many of you must know already. What is it, Chu?"

"Are you going to kill her?" The townspeople looked at Kilaun, eagerly awaiting his instruction. *Like dogs*, Tali thought.

"I am not going to do anything, Chu. This is not my decision. There are no leaders here," Kilaun responded. "But I think that killing her would be against the will of our ancestors." The people nodded in agreement, as if they'd already been thinking it. Tali wasn't certain they wouldn't have nodded with just as much certainty had the answer been different.

Kilaun paused, expecting this answer to be sufficient for Chu and hoping it was the last bump in the road to achieving his aim. Chu was looking at the floor, but had not finished. "Are you to keep her in the mill forever?" Chu asked slowly.

"Certainly you aren't proposing we let her go fetch her army and return?" Kilaun laughed incredulously.

"No, brother. I am not proposing that. I am asking a question. Will you keep her there forever?"

The smile fell off Kilaun's face. His own brother. A half-wit. He'd been backed into a corner. There was tension in the air and the people watched. Tali could hear Soapy holding his breath in apprehension.

"She will remain there as long as necessary to protect this town," Kilaun said flatly, with authority.

"But she is sick, and if you leave her there, she will die," Chu said. "Is that what the ancestors would want?"

A few of the townspeople lowered their heads.

"The ancestors would have put their *family* above their *enemies*," Kilaun said sourly.

"She is not our enemy," Chu said. "She is just a sick and sad woman. It is bad, what you are doing."

Kilaun looked steady and calm. Tali knew him well enough to know he was fuming inside. "Brother, have not all the governments since the Decline proven their fundamental reason to come here as expansion and exploitation?"

Tali winced. Chu wasn't going to do well in a conversation about politics and that was probably exactly why Kilaun asked him the question.

"I...I don't...." Chu stumbled. A little air came back into the room. The argument was at an end, it seemed. But Chu was not done. "I do not know about things like that." Enough time elapsed between each sentence to make the crowd wonder if he was done. "But I can hear the ancestors as well as you can. I only know that it is wrong to let her die. It is the same as killing her. You must let her free."

There was fear in his voice, butut there was also resolve. Tali felt moved by his words. In a room full of supposed equals, the one man who knew himself to be least among them was the only one willing to speak the truth.

Kilaun leaned back and composed his face into one of grave concern. "You have made your point, Chu. I hope that I have made mine. It is not my decision to make. Everyone decides," and with a wave of his hand, Kilaun indicated the townspeople.

"So, my friends, do you agree with Chu, that this Outsider, this representative of a foreign government, a stranger to us all, should go free? Or would you rather not risk the safety and future of your children, your parents, your husbands and wives, for the sake of someone who has never done anything for any of you?"

"It is not your decision then?" Chu asked.

"Dear brother, you know it is not."

Chu looked at the group and said, "Then we will set her free." As Chu had been seated by the front door, he was up and out before his intent could register with the group. He was headed for the mill, of course.

Kilaun remained seated in shocked silence for a moment, then stood up and barked, "Stop him!" forgetting himself.

Soapy, the mechanic, and the metalworker scrambled to follow and ran into the middle of town, blocking Chu's path. Tali and the others rushed out to watch from the porch. It was dark, but the reflection of the moonlight on the snow let their expressions show.

Chu spoke softly but looked directly at the men as he said, "I will not let a woman who has done nothing wrong die. She is sick. She did not hurt any of our people." Nobody moved; the men remained directly in Chu's path.

Chu's voice became less soft. "If you want to kill her, you will have to kill me, too." He stepped closer, and the men were reminded how big he was. Still, their fear of Kilaun was greater than their fear of Chu and they held their ground.

Chu's voice rose to a bellow. "You will kill us both, or she will go free!" With one arm he swept the three men aside and continued in a direct line for the mill.

He pushed inside, disappeared for a minute, and when he returned, he was carrying the woman, who looked sick and afraid. A less frightening person couldn't be imagined. Chu, however, no longer wore the expression of a gentle simpleton. It was clear that there was no room for compromise in him. He would have his way and by force if necessary.

"Brother!" Chu called across the square, the woman dangling in his arms like a rag doll. "She should live with us. In spring, if she wants to leave, she should leave!"

Kilaun was quiet. Tali could see him standing detached at the front of the small crowd. She wondered whether he'd be able to resist having a fit of rage in front of the entire town. He would try to save face, she was sure of it.

"If it is the will of these people, then so she shall. I am not your chief; I am just a person like each of you! What to do with the woman was never my decision to make." Kilaun had quickly rediscovered his inner monk.

"Taliriktug!" Chu called. To her horror, everyone looked at Tali. Her eyes widened. Chu approached her and came close, easily carrying the woman. Some of the men looked edgy.

"You live alone. Will you take her in?" Chu held the woman up toward her like an offering.

Tali looked over at Kilaun. His expression made clear that it was a very bad idea for her to agree to do this. She realized if she did, he would want nothing to do with her.

Salvation.

She could be done with Kilaun without being exiled. It was brilliant. She wanted to kiss Chu on his face, but she stifled her joy.

She did her best to sound reluctant. "I suppose she could. There's my father's old room for her. If...if that's what everyone wants." She saw the woman was shivering. She wanted to cement the decision while momentum was still on her side, so she added, "We can go now."

Chu began walking across town to Tali's house. She didn't dare look at Kilaun. She had to step quickly to catch up with Chu, and so she did. Tali could feel Kilaun's angry eyes burning a hole in the back of her head. And the thought just delighted her.

24

Soapy wasted no time in heading up to Leif's for the horse. He'd done some business with the man a few years back, and he seemed reasonable enough. Soapy was sure it wouldn't be a problem to trade him for a horse, especially once he knew who it was for.

He hiked up the old road, huffing and puffing. It was no easy task to break trail with a foot and a half of snow on the ground. No one had walked this road all winter.

This guy really is a loner.

Now Soapy could respect a loner. He wasn't much of one, but it was something he understood. People sure could be a pain in the ass sometimes. Treacherous even. But Soapy hadn't always had it easy, being such a small man, and he had seen some of the meanness in folks. He had some meanness himself, and he knew that well.

Soapy wondered if this guy had the right idea. It would make things so much easier to not have to deal with his mother, to not be surrounded by people who knew all about every misstep he'd made. People who didn't already think of him as someone undeserving of respect. Being alone sounded good.

But being around people would be better. Being somewhere better, somewhere where he could get a woman, that was what he wanted. That's why he was so quick to jump on this opportunity. Kilaun would surely pay him well, in tobacco and maybe even metal. Maybe he'd get something he could trade to get on a boat headed south.

He was probably the only person in town that wanted to go Outside. Everyone else wanted to keep as far away from the mainland as possible. If they could move further up the valley they probably would. Soapy imagined the mainland, full of people, teeming with life and filth and emotion. He'd take his chances with the savages for a chance at civilization.

These people on the mainland had known real civilization. Kilaun called them savages because in the Decline they'd taken to killing one another. *Survival of the fittest*, Soapy thought. *Plain ol' evolution.* Man liked to pretend that killing wasn't in his nature, but killing's in every animal's nature and Soapy had seen that first hand.

He felt that he hadn't been challenged in the village. He was sheltered, protected, and in a way that he didn't need. His mother gave birth to him down in the Port, back when it was a thriving, healthy town. Soapy'd grown up in this place. He was an Alaskan, whatever was left of that. And what had it gotten him? Sure, he could lay a trap, and split wood, and trudge up a crappy old road like this one breaking snow, but there was no society in which to climb. There was nothing to aspire to, no point beyond mere survival. Kilaun was the only person better off than Soapy in town, and he knew better than to challenge Kilaun's status.

Years ago, at the start of the Decline, Kilaun wasn't yet leader of the village. There was barely a village. Just a few families trying desperately to keep themselves alive and from killing each other. Soapy and his mother had come up there on horse when the Port started becoming dangerous. He was a teenager then, and his mother insisted. Soapy would have stayed and fought it out if he could have. Then he could have made it to the mainland, and become part of something bigger than this. *Bigger than just feeding yourself and waiting for death.*

Kilaun arrived, having come overland. No one came overland. Sometimes Soapy wondered how Kilaun could have actually done it. He came from out east, where they spoke foreign. He looked like the Natives here, though. Dark skin and hair, high cheekbones. *So damn noble.* Soapy wished he looked noble.

So Kilaun shows up one day, just walks right over the mountain like Jesus or something. Says the ancestors led him here. That he had some job to do, and didn't know what it was.

At the time, Soapy was sure that this guy had lost his damn marbles, which would be consistent with walking through the wild of the eastern mountains. Thousands of miles of those mountains, from what Soapy knew, complete with forests with trees bigger than a man could reach around with both arms. Word was that the Decline hadn't bothered the grizzlies none, because they were alive and well and had those thousands of miles of mountainous forests all to themselves. They lived and shit and ripped each other to pieces just fine in those parts, and anyone else that walked through them.

When asked how he made it through without getting mauled to death, Kilaun had responded, "I asked them to be kind." Always with that cryptic shit. Soapy didn't buy it back then, but now he'd seen enough of Kilaun that he figured the son of a bitch probably did just walk clear across the continent, probably didn't even bother with the roads. Just brought his knife and some shoes and went for it, guided by his "ancestors."

Kilaun believed everyone in the village had the same ancestors as him, even though not too many others looked Native like him. That's why he insisted people take traditional names. Supposedly, Kilaun consulted with his ancestors and they told him what the person's spirit name was. A lot of hooey that was. Soapy'd been called something else, but it never took, because people just kept on calling him Soapy. His mother used to be called Janice when he was a child. Now she was called "Chena," although he never figured out what it meant.

No one put up too much of a fuss about the names. They all humored Kilaun. He was giving out names and jobs like some kind of game of pretend, and the people were so desperate for some structure that they went with it.

Kilaun said that it unified them. He said that they were all children just the same, with the same parents, and the names reminded them of that. He said the names meant you are whom you choose to be, not who you were born. Well, that's the way he used to talk anyway. He stayed off that stuff for the most part these days.

In place of the mystical stuff was anger. Kilaun seemed to get worse and worse, and Soapy couldn't imagine why. He had the best job in town – boss of everyone else! No one else had a cook and a maid and a gorgeous wife. Kilaun's brother had come later, by boat Soapy figured, and went to live in the Pass. Guess he didn't have much success out there. Soapy heard they were still starving.

Not in Kilaun's village though. Of all the towns that they'd gotten word of, theirs was by far doing the best. The only real community. Soapy was impressed with what Kilaun had done, but he'd had just about enough of it. He didn't want to haul water on schedule as the town needed it, nor did he want to abide by every one else's wishes for his behavior. He wanted to smoke tobacco and go to bed with women and to be important. He wanted to matter. In the village, they'd always see him as the cook's son.

Soapy saw tracks in the road; they looked like old horse tracks. They came from the opposite direction and went up a trail on the right. He went ahead and headed up the trail, ready to make a deal with the old man in the woods.

25

Chena struggled across the yard hauling water. She was a strong woman, but she was getting old. Chu saw her struggling and went to help.

"You gonna watch me fumble with these all day?"

Chu carried the buckets back to the house for her wordlessly. She emptied them into a barrel and started back toward the spring. Chu walked with her in case she needed help. She didn't seem to like that. She walked faster, but it wasn't hard for Chu to keep up with her.

"You shouldn't'a opened your big mouth," she finally whispered.

Chu remained silent.

"Well, she ain't family and now what. She'll prolly run off, and then what, freeze to death in the woods? Your brother gonna be mad at you for a long time."

They were at the spring and Chu took the buckets from her. She put her hands on her hips and talked as Chu knelt down.

"And to do it in front of all those people!"

Chu broke the flakey ice to make the hole in the surface big enough to sink the buckets in. It was freezing up quick. "That's how Kilaun wants things."

"Never mind that, you still shouldn't'a."

Chu dipped the first bucket in with one hand, like a woman with a ladle – effortless. He stood up, turned, and did the same on the other side.

"Put them up there," Chena said, pointing to the top of the bank. "When you're an old lady like me it won't be so easy to fetch water!"

Chu toted the full buckets to the spot Chena had indicated and set them down for lids. Chena snapped the lids on and let Chu take back the buckets.

"I work all day and then spend all my time worrying about other people, don't have any time to myself!" she ranted.

"I won't ever be an old lady."

"What?"

"You said when I'm an old lady like you."

Chena shook her head sadly. "Chu, you need to think about what you're saying before it comes out your mouth. Or maybe just keep it shut completely." Chena pushed open the back door, letting Chu in. She took the makeshift lid off the rain barrel. He lifted up each bucket and emptied it in.

The cook leaned over and looked in the barrel. "That's enough, Chu."

She leaned against the only stool in the room, caught her breath, and looked at Chu. "You want somethin' to snack on?"

"Ok."

She took a plastic container from on top of a cabinet. She opened it up and let Chu have his pick. It was filled with some sort of a sweet, looked like fudge. Chu took one and popped it in his mouth.

Chena looked him up and down. "You're fast with the water. Why don't you come help me tomorrow with it, when you've got time."

"Ok," Chu responded. He didn't mind helping the cook. She wasn't nice but it gave him a reason to hang around and see Qaniit or Tali. And the sweet was pretty good.

Chu left the kitchen and pulled his coat tight to keep out the cold.

26

It was time to chop wood. The bitter cold had meant he'd used wood faster than he'd have liked, so Leif had fallen behind and his stores were getting low. He no longer had the wiggle room to put off the extra work. Today would be a hard day and he would be a sore old man in the morning.

Leif bundled up, layers on layers, and went out to the barn. He looked at Shadow and her colt, deciding whether it was time to get her back out to work. He needed one horse to go out on his logging trail and pull a sled load of wood back. He figured he'd give Shadow another week or so, as nursing had weakened her. He led Buck out of his stall and put a rope harness on him, and then the small plastic sled.

Out of the corner of his eye and the door of the barn, slightly ajar, he caught a figure passing by. He picked up his axe, clicked for Buck to follow, and led him outside. A person was headed to his house. The person moved like a man but was small like a woman.

Leif watched him silently. The figure turned to the side and Leif could see it was a man. The man was looking around, looking at the chimney, looking at the chicken coop. He was looking entirely too much.

"Hey! Who are you?" Leif shouted. He might be old now, but he was still all gristle, and he wouldn't have some nosey pip snooping about his place.

"Hey there, friend!" the small man responded. He approached Leif across the yard, tromping through the unbroken snow. Leif preferred to use paths than have an entire yard of packed ice. The pip was already annoying.

"I'm here on the orders of commander Kilaun!" he boasted.

"Well, then you can *leave* on behalf of commander Kilaun," Leif retorted, continuing down the path, leading his horse. The small man ran after him.

"No, no, Mister, you should be glad to see me! I've come to trade! Kilaun's got all kinds of stuff you'll be wanting."

"Kilaun's got nothing I want," Leif said. The greasy little man had to trot to keep up.

"No, I doubt that! Food. Hides. Tobacco," the little man was now accounting for the few things Kilaun had to trade. Leif didn't pause. He wrapped Buck's rope loosely around a tree and looked up to survey which trees were good candidates for firewood. He saw a deadwood stand twenty meters away and headed for it.

"Ammo!" the little man continued. Finally, Leif turned and looked at him.

"And what would the mighty Kilaun want from me?" Leif picked a spot on the side of the tree and marked out the top and bottom of his wedge with his axe blade.

"Mister, just one horse. Word has it you've got more than one anyhow." the little man was keeping his distance, probably not wanting to get chopped in half. It was a good thing, because Leif wasn't entirely above whacking someone with the blunt side of an axe. Especially someone who'd just asked him to part with Buck.

Leif pulled back and took a mighty swing. Again. Again. Four swings and he had a perfect wedge in the side of the tree. The little man stood to the side with wide eyes.

"No trade," Leif responded, taking his position behind the tree.

"Surely there's something you'd take for one of the horses?"

Leif's eyes fixed upon his unwelcome guest, and he put both hands on the tree and pushed. It yielded, first whistling, then cracking and finally falling into the snow. Coincidentally, or perhaps not, it toppled in the direction of the would-be trader, who was forced to jump out of the way and wound up gasping as though he'd just run miles.

Leif snorted. "Get on out of here. Kilaun will get nothing from me, traded or otherwise." The horse pawed at the ground.

The little man was getting flustered. Apparently, he did not anticipate that anyone would refuse a request of the mighty Kilaun. Leif was reminded of the many reasons he did not go to town anymore. He looked at the little man and realized he looked familiar.

"Don't I know you?"

"Yeah, I think so."

"A pair of boots for two gallons of fuel," Leif recalled. "That fuel had water in it."

The little man said nothing. He looked like he was panicking. Probably worried about how his master Kilaun would react when he returned without a horse. Leif couldn't care less whether Kilaun threw a temper tantrum. Even if he took it out on this jackass. They were both jackasses.

"Go on, now." He lifted the axe and swung it down on the fell tree. He repeated the effort, until he had his first round of wood.

The small man said, "Come on, Mister, this doesn't have to be hard. Kilaun just wants a horse, you might as well get what you can for it!" If Leif heard Kilaun's name one more time, it might not have been the blunt side of the axe that he used on the man.

"Git," he spat amidst chopping.

He could hear the little man mumbling and cursing under his breath as he turned around and started the trek back to the village.

Leif went back to his chopping, unabated.

27

Libby woke up in a proper bed in a proper bedroom that was confusing and frightening. She'd come to know what to expect in the basement of the mill and, awful though it was, there was comfort in the predictability. Not knowing what torments might be in store for her here made her anxious, though she knew it was better than freezing to death.

There was a night table, a small dresser, a chair, and a lamp. She felt warm, warm in a way she'd all but forgotten was possible.

The curtains were drawn so the room was dark, and the house was completely quiet. Libby slithered out from under the covers and put her feet on the ground. She was wearing socks. They felt kind of big, but warm. She wiggled her toes.

She walked slowly to the window and pulled the curtain back with a bony finger. Snow, and trees, and mountains greeted her. The sun stood behind them all, making things glisten and glitter.

Cold came through the glass, so she let the curtain drop.

The room was meagerly appointed, but it felt friendly. It was neatly kept.

She hazily recalled the night before – was it the night before? The giant carried her here. There was commotion in the town. She wondered if she was safe. The big man painted that picture for her. She wondered if it was still there, decorating the walls of an empty cell. The idea that the cell existed there without her gave her chills. They could put her back in it at any moment.

Now what? Was this the step before execution? Had the big man claimed her for a wife? Would she be set free?

She sat on the bed. She was wearing clothes that weren't hers. They were inside clothes. She vaguely remembered the girl dressing her. But the big man helped her. In other days, such indiscretion might have worried Libby, but she was so thin now, so fragile. She was barely a woman, much less something to be sexualized.

Libby looked at the tin lamp on the nightstand. She could see where someone sanded off the rust spots. It looked old, but cared for.

She gently pulled on the nightstand drawer and peeked inside. A handkerchief, and a few books was all. They looked well read. She picked up the one on top and opened to this passage –

That great and glorious city was damned by the enthusiasm that fueled its rise. Those good men and women who had relished in excess now starved and suffered the worst of fates. Even they could not deny that their anguish was well deserved.

Libby closed the book and put it back in its drawer.

The door handle turned and the door quietly cracked. The girl looked in on her. "You're awake."

"Yes."

She opened the door. "How do you feel?" She tilted her head.

"Okay."

The girl looked concerned. "I've got tea and bread in the front."

"Okay. I'll come out."

The girl nodded and shut the door. She seemed a gentle type.

Libby saw a mirror on the wall next to the door and went to it. She didn't recognize herself. She was so thin, almost gray. She wondered if she was going to die.

Pushing the thought out of her mind, she smoothed her hair down and breathed in. It was clean, dry air, and it didn't hurt her chest. She fumbled with the doorknob and let herself out of the room. She saw she was in a small house, just two rooms it seemed. The girl sat near the fire mending something.

"Did you give me your room?"

The girl put down the cloth and looked up. "No, I sleep out here." She gestured to a palette in the corner. "That was my father's room, but I never could bring myself to stay in it."

The girl stood up and went to the counter. She unwrapped a loaf of bread and cut some thick slices. "Maybe I hope he'll come back," she said, wistfully.

Libby could see that this was a sad sort of girl, probably lonely. She sat down on the rug next to the wood stove and watched the girl in the kitchen. She didn't see the dog quietly approach her until he was sitting right next to her, leaning against her.

"What's your dog's name?" she asked.

"Not my dog. He lives in town. His name's Gun." The dog looked at the girl. "I like it when he hangs around here, though."

The girl got together the bread and some butter, and brought it to Libby. "We eat the same as you've been eating, I'm afraid."

"Before I got here I hadn't had butter for years."

"Really? Why not?" The girl took the teakettle off the stove and poured out two cups. She sat next to Libby on the carpet and eagerly awaited an answer. The dog laid down with his head on her.

"Cows are gone," Libby said in between bites.

"Well what about goats?" the girl said, incredulously. "That's goat butter, there."

"Out east, they've got 'em, but not out west. Still too crazy, I guess. People eat 'em soon as they get there."

They didn't say anything and Libby ate her bread. She watched the girl sip her tea, and noticed she was quite pretty. Such a sad thing to see a lonely, pretty girl.

"What's your name?" Libby asked as she finished the bread.

"Tali."

"I'm Libby."

"You'll get a new name I guess."

Libby looked up apprehensively. There was a hint of what was to become of her in that statement.

"Oh, it's this thing Kilaun does. You get a new name when you start living here. It's like giving people a fresh start. And makes everyone brothers and sisters, I guess. Well that's what he says."

Libby watched the way the girl talked about him. Cooing, almost. Angry at the end. The girl loved him and despised him.

"He's your lover?" Libby asked, without thinking, mouth half full.

The girl looked startled and stood up. Libby sputtered, "I'm sorry--"

The girl grabbed the empty plate and went to the kitchen. The dog stood up and went and lay by the front door.

"I'm the maid," the girl said. "Just the maid."

Libby didn't say anything. The girl let it go.

"I guess I'm going to stay home for a few days to take care of you. Other than food, water, and a warm place to sleep, I wouldn't know what you would need. Is there anything else you think you'll need to start feeling better?"

"Well, am I allowed to leave?"

"Town?"

"The house."

"I don't see why not. Qaniit told me to let you live like anyone else in this town. Although once you get better that means you'll have to do some work." Tali smiled.

"And town?"

"No one comes or goes this time of year."

"And in spring?"

The girl stopped chopping. "I just don't know."

Truth is Libby didn't really want to go back to the mainland. It was shitty there. Having been locked up in a crappy little cell for two months was pretty shitty, too. She wished there was somewhere she wanted to be. She was out of the prison but still a prisoner.

"It'd be nice to take walks," Libby said.

"I'll see if I can't find an extra pair of boots somewhere. Maybe you can borrow the mechanic's wife's boots since she's shut up for a while. I've got enough coats and stuff for the both of us. Worst case scenario, I've still got my father's boots, although they'd be pretty big on you."

Libby finished her tea. "I've gotta go to the bathroom."

"Outhouse round back," Tali said. "Use my boots. They're by the door."

Libby stood up slowly, everything in her body creaking like she'd become an old lady. She walked over to the door and slipped on the boots. The dog got out of the way when she grabbed the handle. She went outside, and Gun followed.

28

Kilaun was not often seen in public in the days following the assembly. Had he accepted the current situation as the will of the people? Most of the townsfolk didn't give it a thought. Of those that did, the concern was buried under the focus on surviving the winter.

Privately, he shifted between pouting, fuming and raging. Inanimate objects felt his violent wrath, but only when he was entirely alone. To be shown up by his half-wit brother in front of everyone, it undid years of work, years spent building an image, earning the trust of the people.

The people. What was the point in earning their trust if they had no interest in doing anything anyhow? Nobody did a thing when Chu stood against Kilaun.

All that was important to them was eating and breeding and making it through the winter. Did they forget that after the winter would come another winter? And another? Survival wasn't only about accumulating firewood and storing food.

And his wife. She had barely looked at him since the assembly. Her silence was worse than laughter. She got what she wanted without lifting a finger. She kept to herself, drawing and reading and curled in front of the fire always doing something that required concentration so she wouldn't have to look at her own husband.

While Kilaun hadn't seen it himself, he was almost sure she was spending time with his brother. She would disappear for afternoons here and there, and she wouldn't take any questions from her husband on where she had been. Or maybe she was at the maid's house. Maybe her betrayal wasn't complete enough, maybe she would work to undermine him even further.

He hadn't given it serious consideration before, but it was possible. His wife had tired of him. And Chu was showing more initiative in leading the town. That nonsense with the prisoner, with him talking to Kilaun like that in front of all those people, was out of control.

Chu. Qaniit. The Maid. Who else? Was it all out of spite? Why were they doing these things?

And where was that horse? Kilaun cared more that he had been denied the horse than that he didn't have the horse. The cook's son, greasy little rat that he was, had assured Kilaun that he'd have the horse here in no time. Kilaun's patience was wearing thin. The horse, perhaps it would help bring his wife back to him.

Kilaun stayed in bed late again. Eventually the cook came in and opened the blinds. Joke was on her, though. The sun didn't come up until late-morning in the dead of winter.

But come up it eventually would. And Kilaun would have four long hours of daylight to wait out until he could hole up in his office for the rest of the night.

He didn't actually *do* anything in his office. He smoked tobacco, and drank tea when it was brought for him. And fumed, and sulked. And wondered where his wife was and what she was doing.

The maid hadn't been around and Kilaun didn't want to see her anyway. That treacherous girl. She should have refused to have the Minarchist in her house. She should have backed Kilaun up. After all the time they spent together, she still couldn't give him that? Such a small thing, and in everyone's interest. Kilaun wished he didn't have to see her at all but he was sure Qaniit would have her back to work soon.

Despite feeling abandoned and supremely lonely, Kilaun wanted no company.

29

Qaniit and Chu went to Tali's house to visit with the stranger. Tali wasn't there, but the stranger answered the door. Libby looked better than before, and she welcomed them inside.

Chu sat with Gun on the floor while the stranger took to tending the stove. It was mid-afternoon, and the fire was waning. Qaniit sat on the rug near the stove. The stranger looked oddly comfortable. Qaniit had anticipated she would be apprehensive, which is why she brought Chu with her.

Qaniit introduced herself and Libby reciprocated. Chu said, "We've met before, but I'm still Chu."

"Hello, Chu," Libby said with a weak smile.

"Are you feeling better at all?" Qaniit asked.

"Yes," the stranger said. "But I wonder when I'll be put back in the cell."

"You won't. I'm sorry we let my husband keep you there as long as we did."

The woman paused in her motions tending the fire as the new information sank in. Her eyes betrayed a nervousness when she turned to face Qaniit.

"Your husband?" Libby asked, and then turned to Chu. "And your brother? He is quite a man. I hope he is kinder to his family than he is to strangers, if you'll forgive me."

"He can be difficult to get along with." Qaniit and Chu looked at one another. Chu had been ostracized from the house since the assembly. He came in quietly late at night just to crawl into bed. Kilaun had been so angry and hostile that no one wanted to be in the house. Only Chena had much to do with him. Qaniit left it to her to deal with him. She had had quite enough.

"Do you want to go home?" Qaniit asked.

"I do."

"We wouldn't know how to get you there."

"I know."

"But you are not a prisoner here now. It's important for you to know that."

Libby looked at Qaniit skeptically, which Qaniit thought understandable given the circumstances.

The woman's apparent doubt and fear brought Qaniit's guilt to surface.

"I am sorry," Qaniit suddenly blurted out. "My husband wasn't always so…." The thought would remain unfinished, though completing the sentence wasn't necessary. "We are still here because of him. We prospered because of him. We've been safe," she said, her speech halting and tentative. "We've had food. There's not physical violence and fear like there is in other places. It might not seem like much of a place to you, but…all the other towns out here… Well, there's not much left."

As Qaniit spoke to the woman, she found herself feeling more and more free. Someone with no allegiances within the town, someone outside of all the complex relationships and interactions, she would see everything freshly, with new and open eyes. Thinking of that perspective caused Qaniit to look upon herself and her town differently. It forced her to evaluate things as an outsider would.

"Maybe…I suppose Kilaun's…change…is part of the cost we've paid. To survive, I mean. That's what you're seeing. It's changed him. Into this." She shook her head in regret. "Or maybe he always was this, and maybe it was hidden from view. I will always wonder if I could have foreseen it. Forestalled it, even." She was surprised by the words emerging from her mouth. She was saying things she hadn't even realized she thought, and she was finding it hard to stop.

"I don't know if it's even possible to take on the kind of responsibility he did and to remain human." She suddenly felt a flood of compassion for the man she'd once loved. Was that man still inside Kilaun, suffering horribly? Was Qaniit herself part of that suffering?

Libby spoke, her voice stronger, more secure and confident than one would expect given her recent suffering. "I understand. I really do. I have seen what responsibility can do to good men. I have seen the paranoia that the horrible things that happen in life can cause. Survival has been hard everywhere," Libby explained. "And it's better than we are doing on the mainland, still."

"This is the best that we know of in these parts," Qaniit continued. "The other towns that remain, from what we know, are bad places. Killing, rape, slavery, starvation. Sickness. Death can come from anywhere at any moment. It's not like that here, and that's mostly a credit to Kilaun.

"Kilaun gave us a place where we could live, and be safe, and make a try for happiness. We all lost family in the decline. All of us. And, now, we have each other. Part of that is Kilaun, who gave us this. We all feel gratitude to him, we really do. But there is fear as well. And his values...well, I suppose they are not shared by all of us." Qaniit did not elaborate that she and Chu were the only people she knew of who questioned Kilaun's values. Perhaps there were others, but she'd seen no evidence of it.

"Now we have to decide whether he can lead us down the path that we want for the future." Saying this caused her to realize that she'd been weighing that exact question for some time.

When Libby next spoke she pushed another question into the smoky air: "But...is he the kind of man who will stand aside if you decide his direction is not the right one?"

Qaniit stared at the floor as they sat silently. Then she looked to Chu. He was stroking the dog. She had suggested to him that he take a role of leadership in the town, not over her husband, but with him.

Chu had not given her much of an answer. He was still upset about having trouble with Kilaun.

Libby closed the stove. The weight of her question had crushed the conversation. There was nowhere left for it to go and so, eventually, Qaniit began again, changing both the subject and her tone.

"The townspeople agree that you should not be held if you really are just an emissary. I believe you. They want to hear it from you. Would you be willing to talk to them?"

"I would."

"In the past, the Outsiders who have come into this region have instilled terror in the villages. They raped, stole, and burned everything in their path. The townspeople here are peaceful. There is regret about what you have been through. There has just been so much fear, and fear makes people act in ways that do not reflect their values."

Libby looked away. "Yes, I have seen that as well," she whispered, as though to herself.

Qaniit was quiet. The fire crackled.

Libby snapped her attention back at Qaniit and continued. "Everyone is fearful. They are like starving dogs. On the mainland, no one trusts each other. Even in the government, you have one or two people who are honorable, who want to establish something good for the people. But most of them are just trying to keep themselves alive and fed, no matter the cost to others. I volunteered as an emissary because I was hoping to find something better. I just wouldn't believe that the entire world was in the sorry state that we were in. It was my only way out." Libby looked at Qaniit in earnest. The stranger seemed to be an honest woman, and Qaniit believed the townspeople would take to her.

"You did not find what you were looking for?" Qaniit asked.

"I sort of did. I was looking for something different, and this is definitely that. I was not looking to be locked up for two months, hungry and cold. I had a lot of time to think.

"I say I want to go home, but I don't know where home is anymore. I'm afraid of your husband and I want to be somewhere safe, but in truth I'm not sure there's anyplace safer than here for me. The place that I grew up is gone, burned and used and gone. The government I came here working for might or might not exist at this point. I want to go someplace else, same as I did when I was there, but there is no place else to go."

In a flash, Qaniit realized that is how she had felt, too, wanting to go somewhere else, but with no place to go. But she didn't feel that way anymore. Now she wanted to stay.

It was Chu, she realized. His company, his moral compass, it gave her hope for a world that she might want to live in. Qaniit found she was smiling but her expression was not appropriate to the conversation. She quashed the smile that Libby did not seem to have noticed.

"I will make sure you are safe for as long as you want to stay here," Qaniit said, directly and sincerely.

"Thank you."

Qaniit felt that they understood each other.

"I happen to know a rather large man who is willing to do the same," Qaniit said. The two women looked over at Chu. They had both been speaking as though he weren't there or listening. He remained quiet but Qaniit thought she noticed him blushing at the attention.

"Thank you for helping me, Chu," Libby said. She spoke like she was talking to a child. Qaniit was sure Chu didn't notice. He knew when someone was sincere, and didn't care about the other things. He was how Qaniit wished her husband could be.

"I brought you something," Chu said to Libby. Qaniit raised her eyebrows. She knew nothing about this. He stood up, pulling a piece of wood out of his jacket, and bringing it over to Libby.

Libby took it and, looking at it, started to cry.

"I'm sorry," Chu said, worried.

"No, it's okay," she said, wiping her face. "I really appreciate it. Thank you." Libby stood up and hugged him.

He hugged her back. "You're welcome, Libby." She looked so very small wrapped in his arms. Qaniit swallowed and fought her own impulse to cry. She felt so disappointed with herself, and so proud of Chu for having stood up to Kilaun. This woman was becoming a real person to Qaniit right before her very eyes. To Chu, in his simplicity, she had been a real person from the beginning.

Qaniit looked down and saw Chu's painting. There were holes in the corners from where it had been nailed into the wall, and it was a little wet from where snow that had been stuck to it had melted. Chu was seemingly the only person in the village who could feel. And he had allowed Qaniit to feel again as well. She wiped the tears forming in her eyes unashamedly.

30

He'd tried it the easy way but some people couldn't be reasoned with. To get what you want, sometimes you have to take it. One thing Soapy wanted was respect. Another was a horse. The man would part with neither. Soapy would do what he had to do.

Leif. Soapy knew his name and he burned red at the thought of it. Soapy kept replaying their encounter in his mind, growing angrier at each successive review. That the man would send him back to Kilaun humiliated and empty handed was bad enough, but the absolute lack of respect he'd shown was unacceptable. Hell, that falling tree could've killed Soapy.

Soapy would never allow himself to be treated that way again.

Leif was even bent out of shape over that trade years ago. This was someone who could never be happy. Water in it? Soapy wanted to trade it, not use it, and it wasn't as if he'd had anything to test it on, so it wasn't his fault.

Besides, fuel was rare and valuable, and the old man had gotten a deal on it. A few gallons for an old pair of rabbit boots! Even back then, it had been a steal. It'd been years since any fuel had been in the area. Half a decade? More? Soapy couldn't remember. There wasn't any fuel any more, that was for sure. Those few gallons he traded to the old man might have been the last fuel Soapy would ever see.

Soapy trudged up toward the glacier toe by the light of the moon. He'd waited for a clear night so he wouldn't have to use a lantern. The moonlight reflected off the snow, which now thickly blanketed everything – the ground, the trees, the rocks. One big fluffy carpet of white. It'd been so cold recently that it stayed pure powder.

Soapy had dressed as warmly as possible. It'd taken him the entire day to get up to the old man's and back when he went the last time. And now, with the recent snow and his wanting to be sure to be careful with his tracks, he figured it'd take double. He had left the village a couple hours after dusk, which came somewhere around mid-afternoon this time of year. There were still a couple weeks until winter solstice, but the days were already damn short.

The lack of daylight worked to his advantage for a mission like this, but the bitter cold of a long night made the journey itself frightening. It would be ten or twenty below for the entire trip. He donned snowshoes and carried a light pack. He walked parallel to the old road so that any tracks he left would be concealed. He snickered every few minutes, as he was very impressed with his own cleverness.

But the miles wore on him, and Soapy became far less enthusiastic about the trip, despite enjoying the opportunity to sneak around. His teeth chattered, his toes burned cold, and the legs on his pants were frozen solid.

The little man was in the process of reviewing the reasons he had to feel sorry for himself as he crossed a stream that appeared well frozen, but the ice broke where it was hollow underneath. As he sensed his footing giving way, he felt the terror of death. His leg reached the bottom of the hollow area and smashed the second layer of ice, which promptly also cracked, immersing his feet in water. It was just deep enough to put water in his boots and soak his pants nearly to his knees. Soapy managed to get a thickly gloved hand onto some sturdy snow to keep from toppling over entirely.

To be wet in that cold was death. Soapy just about ran the instant he emerged from the water, fully gripped by panic. He begged no one in particular for his life, and tears froze at the bottoms of his eyes.

By the time Soapy got within a mile of the old man's house, he still had not settled on a course of action. It was colder than he'd expected and he couldn't feel his toes at all anymore. He clenched and unclenched his fingers, but it wasn't helping. There was no way he'd make it back all the way like this, especially going a roundabout way so as not to leave evidence of his intended theft.

He stood at the edge of Leif's land, and looked between the cabin and the barn, considering his options. He could steal the horse like he planned, and probably freeze to death on the way back to the village. Or he could go throw himself on the old man's mercy and get himself warm and out of danger.

Hell, Leif would know what he was there for. Leif might be no less likely to kill him than the cold.

The moon said it was well past midnight. There were no lights in the cabin, but there was smoke from the chimney. Damn it! If he went over there, how could he steal the horse after that? The old man would be onto him for sure. He didn't care if the old man knew just for the sake of it, but he didn't want him coming into town and making a commotion. That could wreck any goodwill he'd earned with Kilaun and Kilaun's favor was a precious commodity.

No, he had to see this thing through. He agreed to do a job for Kilaun, and this would be his only opportunity to fulfill that commitment. It was his only chance to better his situation that so that he could finally get the hell out of the village. He had to find a way to get to the mainland, and if he faced a little shivering and teeth chatting beforehand, well, that was a small price to pay.

With that thought, Soapy headed toward the barn.

31

That night, the ancestors gave Kilaun a dream.

He was in his village, which was empty. The sun beamed bright and it was summer. The trees were still, as if there were no wind at all. Nature made no sounds. Kilaun walked in the silent picture.

Kilaun saw his own home across the square and walked on a path of stones toward it. The grass grew very tall around the house, taller than he had ever seen it. The blades were thick, like the grass in the plains he saw during his long journey years ago. Those blades brushed coarsely against him as he tried to keep on the stones.

But the stones grew smaller and smaller, and farther apart, and he found himself tangled in razor-sharp blades of stiff grass that he could feel making many cuts on his arms. Kilaun walked forward and did not look down, but he could feel blood starting to drip from the cuts.

He reached the porch, which was empty. It did not have any of the things that his porch usually had on it. No benches, no boots, no wind chimes, no tools. He recognized it as his own porch, but also saw the strangeness.

The wood did not respond to his steps. It did not creak or give, and it did not bend, even slightly. Kilaun knew it was not wood at all, but something else pretending to be wood.

He entered the house, which was his house, but not, and he was disoriented. He walked down the hall and into the first room he came to, which was the guest room. It did not look like his brother stayed in this room at all. Instead, it was empty and bare.

Kilaun lay down on his back on the guest bed. He looked at the ceiling that looked back at him, quietly and without judgment. Out of the corners of his eyes, he saw the world giving way.

Out the window, he saw that the blackberry bushes were growing, quicker than he'd ever seen. First, a single vine grew up one window, then a few more. The other window, next – a vine growing high, then another and another. The blackberry plants grew and grew until so many vines covered the windows that Kilaun could not see outside anymore. He was lying on his back, now unable to move. The plant kept growing until the light was closed out altogether and Kilaun found himself in darkness.

His dream perspective changed and he was looking down on his own body lying in the bed, in the darkness created by the bushes, and he could see that the vines covered all the walls and the roof.

The pace accelerated and the entire world grew quickly, in a fervent sprint.

Mushrooms popped up out of the ground and grew on the stumps and on the trees. Mushrooms of all different sizes. There were little, tiny ones, with strange patterns and shapes. There were large ones that looked fluffy and warm and friendly. And the little ones grew big and the big ones grew little, and everything teemed with life and growth and suffocation.

Kilaun looked down on himself, through the vines then through the roof, and a single mushroom grew out of the center of his body's forehead. He watched the eyes on his body go wide with horror. He knew that the man he was looking at in the bed could not move, but only because he was watching. He was no longer in that man's head.

Out of each of the cuts on the body's arms, blood poured out, soaking the handsewn quilt, soaking it until the entire thing was soaked through and through, bloody in the darkness. Blood ran off the corners of the saturated quilt in a steady stream. Kilaun was aware in that dreamlike way that the floor merely looked like wood, but it was false, and it held the blood like stone. The blood spread across the floor until it was entirely covered with a single, unbroken surface on glistening red.

The smell of exsanguination woke the blackberry vines. They became predatory and reached for the blood, pushing at the windows, trying to find cracks in the walls, determined to enter the room. The vines tore at the wood siding, pressed in between the panels, pulling, tearing, frantic to get in. Nails fell from the walls, boards creaked, crevices grew, as did the body's terror as the vines pushed their way in.

At first, the vines ignored the Kilaun that Kilaun was watching from above. It was the blood pooled on the floor they wanted. But that quickly grew scarce, and the seething vines searched and searched until the pool of blood had been completely exhausted. They started crawling the walls and seeking the source. They found the man on the bed with wide frightened eyes, mushroom sprung from his weathered forehead, and grass-induced cuts crisscrossed along his arms.

The vines started crawling up and down the man's body, feeling against his face, feeling against his clothes and skin. They fumbled about his cuts and his mouth and his ears and his rectum, and all the other ways they might access the inside of his body and the source of the blood.

In a concert of movement, each vine tore at Kilaun, but not in a soulless plant-like way; there was rage in their effort. They opened him up and pressed into him. Every cut on his arm, every hole, each of his fighting eyes, they were all subject to the siege.

The vines entered him and wandered through his veins, drawing all his blood out, making him a shell of a living thing.

As quickly as they had entered, they sucked the shell empty and dry. The blackberry vines went quiet again and lay in peace, tangled up inside the dried out husk of a man.

32

Chena had never really thought much of her son, so her suspicion was that he'd done something spectacularly stupid when she saw how filthy his feet were and how he scrubbed them.

More disappointing to her than his ineptitude was his lack of hardiness. He certainly didn't handle discomfort or pain like a man should. She'd seen infants more stoic. At moments like this, Chena wondered how Soapy could possibly be her son. She was strong, and wouldn't have let out even a peep if she'd gotten her toes frozen, nor would she have been so stupid as to allow it to happen. She stared at her son with contempt.

Soapy came home in the morning twilight, caked with ice and crying for help. She'd thought of not helping, letting the boy fend for himself for once, hoping he'd learn a lesson, but she now viewed him as beyond hope, so she helped, making sure to let him know just how much he was inconveniencing her. She heated up some water and started thawing out her boy's feet. She knew from experience that it doesn't hurt much to freeze your toes, but it sure hurts like hell to thaw them out.

What he was doing off traipsing through the countryside in the middle of the night in the dead of winter? That kind of behavior was enough to get a person killed. She thought even he was smarter than that. She had half a mind to go and tell Kilaun what she thought of him sending her son off into the night like that, but of course that assumed that Soapy's claim of being on an errand for Kilaun was correct. And it would be assuming that Soapy had properly interpreted the wiser man's instructions. Some kind of miscommunication seemed likely given her son's involvement and the obvious stupidity of being out in the middle of the night in the middle of winter. Kilaun was no fool but she couldn't say the same of her son. Of course, the only way she'd ever know what was going on was by talking to Kilaun himself.

But Kilaun hadn't been right in the head himself as of late, and Chena figured that on this particular occasion she didn't want to make things more difficult than they needed to be. He'd know well enough that she wasn't happy with him when she wasn't there to bring him tea that morning. Maybe the maid and Kilaun would finally have to stop avoiding each other.

She spent an hour on Soapy's feet when he got home, trying to work the blood back into them. It wasn't looking too good for his right foot, and she was thinking he'd probably lose the little toe, and maybe the next one up. Just what she needed – a crippled son! One would think that in his thirty-odd years of life that he would've figured out how to stop being a jackass. No such luck. *Well, maybe a crippled son would better mind his mother's suggestions.*

Chena put Soapy in her bed since it was nearer the fire. Around mid-morning Qaniit stopped by to make sure everything was all right since Chena hadn't showed at the house.

Chena told her the god-honest truth, that Qaniit's no-good husband sent Soapy on some vague errand that left him with frozen feet, and that meant Chena'd be home all day caring for his useless self and that if Kilaun wanted her at work then he ought come over and start massaging Soapy's toes because the boy was in no condition to be doing that hisself.

Qaniit left without asking more.

Chena set to fixing some stew and kept Soapy warm and bundled, and tended to his jacked up feet. She felt it was a mother's duty, whether she liked it or not.

33

Qaniit came back from Chena's house and found Tali in the kitchen cleaning.

"Kilaun still in bed?"

"I haven't seen him this morning."

"Would you wake him, then?" Qaniit asked.

"I—" the girl stammered.

"No. It's fine. I'll get him." Qaniit sighed deeply. She didn't prefer to deal with her husband but she wasn't going to force Tali to deal with him. Tali's response to the request said plenty about how the girl felt about Kilaun. At least Qaniit had the power of status on her side. The help had to deal with Kilaun and didn't even have the luxury of ignoring him.

Qaniit went into the bedroom and found it dark. She pulled back the curtains, announcing, "Get up, Kilaun."

But the room was empty and silent. Even though it was early, she checked his office. Nothing. Puzzled, she went back over to the kitchen.

"He's not there," she told Tali.

Tali stopped cleaning and cocked her head. "Not there?" Her eyes darted about, as though Kilaun were hiding.

The women looked at one another. Kilaun had been acting increasingly strangely, and even sleeping late. Qaniit could not even remember what he used to do when he got up at a decent hour.

"Well maybe he's getting back to his old self," Qaniit proposed.

Tali shrugged uncomfortably and got back to work. The girl seemed different lately. Qaniit was trying to think what might be wrong with the girl when the sound of her name came booming through the house. Kilaun.

Qaniit felt anger rise in her in preparation for a battle.

Qaniit hastily made her way into the great room and stared at her husband, who smiled dumbly at her in a manner entirely unlike him. "Did you make Chena's boy nearly freeze to death by going out in the middle of the night?"

Kilaun looked befuddled momentarily, but the smile returned.

"Well, my dear, he's certainly too old to be called a boy at this point, and I didn't intend for him to endanger himself, but I did have him perform an errand for me. Or perhaps it would be more accurate to say that it was for you. A present, from me, to my beautiful wife."

Qaniit was puzzled but tried not to let it show. Her husband would unmercifully pounce on any weakness. A cheerful Kilaun was certainly not something she expected.

"A present." She was confused, but there was not the slightest hope within her that he was sincere.

"Come, my darling. I hope you like it." He spoke through a wide grin. She began to consider the possibility that his smile was genuine rather than a ploy. When he gently guided her out into the doorway, she saw the horse.

She recognized it instantly. One of Leif's, of course, for where else could you get a horse? She was dumbfounded, the idea of a present forgotten, nonetheless overcome by the unexpected presence of the powerful and majestic beast, which stood there indifferent to both of them, pawing at the snow.

Then sudden thought of Leif, here in town, flashed into her head, here with Kilaun half out of his mind for the last week, month, year, and panic rose in her.

She looked around. "Where is he?"

"Where is who?"

"Leif."

"The old man? Probably at his place." Kilaun looked at her and responded to the concern on her face. "Oh, you thought—! No, no. I traded for the horse. For you."

It took several moments for this idea to sink in for Qaniit.

"For...for me?" she stepped out of the doorway to see the horse better. The emotional remnants of her journey up the valley with Leif pushed their way into her consciousness. He had always been so kind to her, so generous. She recalled that Shadow had just had a colt, but was still surprised that he traded Buck, no matter what Kilaun had offered him. Buck was the horse that had carried her up to this place.

And for Kilaun to swallow his pride, to offer to do business with Leif even though they stood so far apart, to do something kind, to do something for her... it made her question so much of the way she'd been viewing things lately. That he could know just the right thing for her and that he could make it happen? Her eyes grew moist.

Her expression had softened dramatically. "What's the occasion?" she asked him, still looking at the horse.

He grabbed her by the shoulders and faced her toward him, looking in her eyes. "The occasion is that you are my wife. I want you to have the things that make you happy. I want you to be happy."

At that moment, she saw the man she married and it was good to see him again. Without thinking, she wrapped her arms around him and thanked him for his gift. She kissed him in a way she had not kissed him for years. With passion, honesty, and love. For that moment, she felt married again.

Qaniit let go of her husband and ran over to Buck, climbing on up without bother of a blanket. She took off through the village, not caring about the townspeople looking at her like she was mad, not caring about the burn in her thighs from holding on, not caring about the long winter. She ran the horse up the logging trail and down the backside of town. When she completed her short circuit, she was already out of breath. She hopped off and smiled big at her husband.

"Thank you," she said, feeling like a very lucky woman indeed.

That night, Qaniit went with her husband to the bedroom, for the first time in nearly a year. Her intimacy was sincere and, when she kissed him, it rang true. Kilaun was very glad to have her back.

34

Tali cleaned the cabin and prepared to receive visitors. Chu had invited some of the townspeople to come and talk to Libby. She was willing to receive them and this was supposed to make everybody feel more comfortable. Libby being in the house made things feel homier. Like a family. It was something Tali had missed since her father had died.

The mechanic and his wife came with their new baby, and the lumberman's wife but not the lumberman, and the girl Sila because she was feeling curious, and of course Chu was there which was comforting no matter how little he said. Mercifully, Chena stayed away, as her son had apparently taken ill and she was caring for him. Qaniit and Kilaun were not there either. Qaniit didn't want anyone to feel like she was there as an authority figure, and no one told Kilaun.

The visiting was awkward at first. People weren't used to talking to anyone they hadn't known for years. Nor were they used to gatherings without Kilaun to lead the proceedings, so it began with self-conscious silence.

Tali took her time serving tea, feeling somewhat apart from the awkwardness while she had something to do. She imagined it must've been horrifying for Libby, thinking that these people were partly responsible for her fate. But it picked up soon enough.

Chu, clearly uncomfortable speaking to so many, spoke with all the grace and confidence of a newborn calf taking its first steps. He stuttered and stammered at the outset and his voice even cracked like a teenager's at one point. But people were just happy to have someone speak and Chu took the pressure off. Eventually, he managed to string some coherent sentences together that focused on Libby and how she wasn't a newcomer anymore because she'd with them for several months and wasn't it time they all got to know her a little bit?

Tali couldn't help smiling when Chu spoke. He was so unreservedly himself. It was impossible not to like him.

The lumberman's wife spoke next. "I'm Janij, and we haven't met but I did want to say, well, I guess welcome to our village. I hope things are going all right for you and I, for one, don't mind that you're here."

Libby nodded. "Thank you Janij. It's nice to meet you. I'm Libby." She addressed the entire room.

"Nice to meet you, too," and the lumberman's wife sat down. "Oh, I'm sorry my husband couldn't be here," she noted, and then sank back against the wall. The group returned to clumsy silence as everyone pondered how she did not offer an excuse for her husband's absence.

And so it was left to Chu again to move things forward. "Libby, do you think you could introduce yourself to everyone?" In the end, it was only Libby that could make them comfortable with her anyhow.

"Hello everyone, I'm so pleased to meet you all. I suppose you all know I'm from the mainland. It's hard there and I just came up hoping for a place where I could live safely and not go hungry."

Tali frowned. This wasn't true. She knew that Libby had come up as an emissary for the foreign government. Libby must be worried about what people heard, like there were too many ears listening to be completely honest.

"Did you come up for the government?" the mechanic asked. Tali saw his wife trying to shush him but having no such luck. "Did you come up to make us join?"

Libby thought and looked at the mechanic.

"I don't know anymore. I thought I was coming up here for contact, so that my government and your leaders could share information or resources. But now I see that you all aren't that much different."

"What's that supposed to mean?" he asked.

"Just that you all don't have more resources than we had. You have more food, but that's food that has to be consumed here, food that doesn't leave."

"What do our resources matter?"

"I think that's why they sent me up here," she said, plainly.

"They sent you up here to find out about our resources? Why? Are they going to send people to follow? Will they try and take from us?" The mechanic was getting upset and his nerves were contagious.

Libby looked tired. She still wasn't fully recovered. She just kind of shrugged. Tali looked at Chu, hoping he would step in and patch this up.

"She hasn't done anything wrong. She shouldn't be treated poorly," he said.

Tali piped up, "She's been a very good person to live with. She is kind and promised not to do anything that would harm the town. Right, Libby?"

Libby nodded, but she was falling out of it.

"Well, do you want to stay?" the lumberman asked.

"I don't know," Libby answered. "I just want to live. And not have it be so... hard." The townspeople didn't say anything. Libby wanted the same thing that everyone wanted. For as long as someone still wanted to live, they were doing all right. But that wasn't always easy.

The meeting kind of died down. No one really wanted to talk. Winter was a little funny on the soul sometimes and, this time of year, people tended to be quiet anyway. Tali put out some snacks and people ate a little, but overall the event wasn't as much of a success and she had been hoping.

Libby sat quietly, not talking too much and not being talked to. Tali sat by her when she could, when she was not serving or seeing someone out. Chu had to go do chores. Chena had appointed him interim water hauler while she was off duty taking care of Soapy.

It wasn't long before everyone had left and the house was quiet again.

"I appreciate what you tried to do, Tali. I'm sorry I couldn't say what they needed to hear." Libby sat with her knees to her chest in front of the fire.

Tali went and sat next to Libby and gently leaned against her. "No, no, no, it's all right. They'll come around."

"Ok."

Neither of them believed it, however.

35

Leif armored himself against the cold in preparation for the trip to town. Leif knew his horses. The instant Buck wasn't where he was supposed to be, Leif knew, and rage flooded his mind. He would have Buck and he would have vengeance as well. This was about survival.

He'd been wrong to be so dismissive of Kilaun's vile little minion. Not that he regretted his treatment of the buffoon, but he knew he shouldn't have just considered it over and done with. Certainly, if Kilaun had sent him, it was for a reason.

Kilaun. The man hated him, he knew that, but that he'd show him this kind of disrespect was shocking. Perhaps Kilaun had become even more unhinged. It was a frightening thought. But, if he took the horse, what would he take next? Permitting it was not an option and this Leif saw clearly even through his rage.

The walk to town was a long one and bloodlust occupied Leif's mind for most of it. Seemingly every scenario that was possible in combat between he and Kilaun played out in his mind. Sometimes Kilaun had the upper hand and sometimes it was

Leif. Deep down Leif knew he had no desire to kill another man, even Kilaun, but with the village still hours away he indulged himself by picturing smashing an inert Kilaun's skull with a stone or looking in his eyes while grinding his boot into the man's larynx.

But, there were other villagers. Children, even. The thought sobered him and the ecstasy of rage gave way to the grim knowledge that there was no clean way for this to end.

Shadow had been well ready to start riding again, but Leif didn't want to take her. He was gonna get Buck and ride him back. Besides, if there was trouble, he didn't want to have her tied to some tree in the village. He didn't plan to get himself killed, but he was mad enough to risk it, so he left their stalls open just in case. Given the weather, the horses wouldn't leave unless they needed to.

Kilaun had stepped well over the edge of civilized behavior with this stunt. He'd never have imagined that with all Kilaun's pride he'd stoop to stealing. And that little pip had served as his tool and dared to come on Leif's property like that in the middle of the night. Leif traveled a long way to get away from that kind of mess on the mainland, and he wasn't about to put up with it all the way out here.

By the time he got to town, he had been stewing for the good three hours it took him to walk the old road. He stopped for a minute on the edge of town, breathed deep, and decided on a course of action. He would go right to the center of town and raise hell until his horse was standing right there in front of him again. He might have been an old man, but Leif still remembered how to raise hell. He had brought his gun just in case, although he had so little ammo that he didn't want to use it.

Leif started walking hard with this goal in mind, knowing that he probably looked like a mad man. He'd been out on his own for years now, and in the bush it didn't matter what you looked like. A wild beard, torn clothes, a dirty face – when it came time to look crazy, being a bushman became a benefit.

He was stomping along, getting closer to the quiet town square, when he heard a woman's voice calling from behind him.

"Leif!"

A woman stood on the porch of a house. It was a house Leif had once known well, the house of a friend, dead some years now. The young woman was very pretty and looked very pleased, but how did she know him? He took several steps toward the porch, and as his less than perfect vision was given an easier task, he found her face familiar. "Leif, it's you," the woman said breathlessly, and yes, her voice, it was familiar too, but…how? It took a few moments for him to piece it all together: The house, the voice, the familiar face, and the years that had passed. She had been a little girl. Taliriktug.

He felt stunned, incapacitated. The idea that this person was someone he'd been close to, that she was so changed, was more than he could comprehend in just a few moments. The rage was pushed from him and forgotten for the moment.

"Tali?" Leif took his hat off. Frigid air rushed his sweaty scalp.

"I thought that was you. You look like a snake bit you!"

Leif felt shy, for this was not the Tali he knew. She was lovely, even if she was the daughter of a friend. And he suddenly felt ashamed of his appearance. Looking like a madman hadn't seemed like a problem just minutes earlier, but who knew he'd be talking to someone he cared for, someone young and beautiful, someone who remembered him in better years.

He lowered his head and searched for something to say. He'd never considered himself good with words even when he'd lived among other people. The solitude hadn't helped.

"What are you doing here, Leif? No, wait...." The woman who had been a girl remembered her manners. "Please, come in out of the cold, I'll make some tea, let's talk. Oh I'm so pleased to see you!" Leif managed to be both pleased and frightened by her minor burst of emotion.

She headed in the door and beckoned for him to follow and so he trod slowly up the stairs, suddenly and for the first time in a long while conscious of every last thing about himself and how he might be perceived.

The cabin seemed as familiar as if he'd just left it yesterday. It wasn't much, but Tali kept it well enough. It was clean and cozy and he felt much like he did in the old days to be there, as though he were among friends. She bade him sit and he took his place near the fire. His body was cold and his legs were tired and he hadn't really noticed until now. Tali fixed some tea.

When was the last time someone made him tea? The idea of being taken care of seemed both foreign and freeing. His hands fidgeted despite the hours of exertion he'd just endured.

Genuine curiosity about her life overcame his self-consciousness, and so he spoke. "You live alone now?"

"Yes, well, sort of. I mostly do but just recently this woman from the Outside started staying here."

"Oh, Qaniit told me someone came. So Kilaun let her free then?"

"Actually, he didn't," Tali whispered as she handed him a cup. "Careful it's hot," she warned. She'd been a gossip even as a girl, which Leif didn't mind because he liked hearing about things without having to ask. And now there were so rarely things to hear about.

She sat down and continued, "Kilaun's brother let her out. He's been in town scarce a few months now. Kilaun wouldn't let her out, was just gonna let her sit in there until the end of time I guess. His brother, well he's none too bright, but I don't know. He's just different. He figured we couldn't leave her locked up if she didn't even do anything wrong. Apparently him and Qaniit both tried to get Kilaun to let her out, but Kilaun said he wouldn't and that if anyone had something to say assembly'd be the time."

How long since Leif had heard a new story? He'd forgotten about the horse, his jaw was slack, his eyes wide, and he'd not tasted a drop of his tea.

She took a deep breath, as though in anticipation of her next sentence taking a long while. "Assembly came and Kilaun said 'Oh, it's the town's decision,' like he always does and then just talks a lot and somehow no one decides at all, it's still just whatever he says. But Chu, the brother, you know, he hasn't been here long, he just spoke right up, just like Kilaun says he wants. Maybe he doesn't know better. He doesn't seem very smart.

"Anyhow, he says 'No, that ain't right,' or something like that in front of *everybody,* and they argued and so on. So Chu, he's real big, way bigger than Kilaun, he said it wasn't right and he marched right across the square and came out the old mill carrying Libby in his arms like a baby! She was so skinny then. To see her like that, though, looking like a rag doll, everyone knew that it wasn't right to just have her locked up in the mill even if now that she's out maybe she'll go and tell the Outsiders where we are. So I said I'd take care of her here and she's doing much better now. I'm fattening her up. She's out for a walk right now, prolly'll come back soon though."

There were so few people Tali was comfortable around, people without agendas, people she knew cared for her. She was surprised at the way the words had poured out of her, at her total lack of self-consciousness while telling Leif the story.

He'd said nothing and his mouth wore only a thin smile, but his eyes made clear how it felt to see her again.

Neither said anything for several moments, though the silence was not awkward.

"It's good to see you," he finally said.

"Good to see you, too." She smiled. "How come you never come visit anymore?"

Leif let out a big sigh. "Oh, Tali, you know why. I just can't deal with all this." His face grew dark. He remembered Buck. He remembered Kilaun. The change in him was evident.

"I wish you could," she said. "It would be so much better with you around."

Leif didn't respond. He wished he could see her more often. Maybe he could. But that was a consideration for another time.

"So why you here now?" she asked, a hint of fear in her voice. Leif's face told a story, and even without that story she knew only something very serious could be the reason for his visit.

Leif's anger built for several moments before he responded. "I came for my horse. Kilaun had his little pet weasel steal it."

"Steal? That doesn't sound like Kilaun." Her voice was plainly skeptical and she shook her head in disbelief. "Are you sure?"

"Kilaun sent Chena's little mutt out to ask me to trade, but I said no. Not only am I not trading my horse, but I'm not doing the slightest favor for that tyrant."

"Soapy? Why would Kilaun send him? Why would Kilaun even want a horse?" She paused for a moment. "It's all very strange."

"Kilaun hasn't been acting right for a while now," Tali said quietly. "I wouldn't think he'd have stolen, though. You sure your horse is here?"

"Well, I'm gonna find out."

The door swung open and a bundle of coats with a face buried deep inside it appeared, outlined by the white world outside. Leif remembered his wife from many years ago.

The woman stamped the snow off her boots and unbundled. So many layers, it was impressive. But an Outsider would have thinner skin than someone who'd spent some winters there.

Tali tended to the fire and Leif watched the woman situate herself. She was somewhere around 45 years old and she was someone who'd seen some things. Her face had its share of creases and sadness, but it was a gentle face, and Leif thought it lovely. When he realized he was staring, he had the thought that he didn't get out enough. Staying holed up there in the woods and he fell in love with any woman he laid eyes on.

"How was your walk?" Tali asked.

"Oh, just fine." The woman noticed Leif for the first time.

Tali introduced them. "Libby this is Leif. Leif, Libby. Leif was close friends with my father. He lives about a half-day's walk from here."

"Well nice to meet you." Libby came over and shook his hand. She shook it firmly, like a woman in the military. Leif's wife had been in the military.

"Likewise."

"You seen a horse out there, Libby?" Tali asked.

"Heard of one," Libby responded, heading to the kitchen area. "Chu said Kilaun got one. I asked him where it came from and he didn't know."

"Came from my damn house!" Leif said, forgetting himself.

Tali explained to Libby, "Leif says Kilaun stole his horse."

"I don't just *say* he stole my horse. He stole my damn horse!" Leif said.

"Leif, please be careful," Tali told him. She wanted to remind him that Kilaun was bigger, stronger, younger and more likely to have allies but thought better of it, figuring that by injuring his pride she might only lead to him acting even more rashly.

"Alright."

And with that, Leif took his leave. Tali felt as though she'd been reacquainted with a long lost part of her past, something from her father's time, and desperately hoped the reunion wouldn't be the prelude to mourning.

36

Kilaun may as well have been glowing, he felt so joyous after Qaniit came and offered herself to him. He didn't know how long it had been since they'd been together in that way and he made a point of not speculating based on a guess that he would not like the answer.

It had been passionate, nothing like with the servant girl. Kilaun found himself unable to help smiling. He felt he could best prolong his euphoric state by going up to the ridge, which had been a reliable pleasure for him over the years, unlike his wife's affections.

The dream the ancestors had sent him had been hanging over his head before Qaniit came to him and, while she'd provided a welcome reprieve from the dark thoughts it had prompted, they returned as he ascended to the ridge. He felt as though the village was on the brink of something and he could not risk ignoring or misunderstanding the wisdom offered by those who came before him.

Kilaun's long legs ate up the mountainside in great chunks. Climbing always made him feel strong. It was the first time he had come up this way since the last few snows. The trail was thick and difficult but he never doubted his ability to make it and, just as the thought often occurred to him after a climb, he pondered that nobody else in the village could have made it. Kilaun was the strongest.

But... perhaps Chu could. He hadn't made the ascent often since Chu's arrival and it had never occurred to him that he might no longer be without physical peer in the village. Kilaun dismissed the thought, though it counteracted some of the positive energy he felt from his hike.

Winded, he brushed off his rock, sat upon it, and let the thoughts come to him the way they could only when immersed in the solitude provided by this place.

The wind blew cold, but it felt good to be in the open air again. He'd been so crowded recently. Winter was always restricting, but this one felt particularly oppressive. The cook always dragging him out of bed, his wife skulking about avoiding him, his avoiding the maid whose presence reminded him of her unexpected betrayal. And, of course, there was the very disturbing behavior of his brother. Sometimes Kilaun tried to convince himself that Chu simply didn't know any better, but he always returned to the conclusion that his brother was intentionally subverting him.

He'd always taken his brother for a dimwit, but it appeared as though he might need to look closer. Perhaps Chu's big, clumsy façade was just that – a façade. Was he just waiting all these years for an opportunity to take advantage of Kilaun's initiative? Even to Kilaun, that sounded unlikely.

At the time when Kilaun was called out west, Chu had received no such calling. He wanted to tag along on the trip and finally Kilaun was starting to see why. If Chu had stayed east, he might have gotten ripped to shreds by the ensuing lawlessness like everyone else. He certainly wouldn't have been able to build something. At best, he'd be waiting out the disorder like all those other humans. Just waiting.

That was not Kilaun's way, though. The ancestors gave him the opportunity to trek out west and he listened. He was willing to listen, he was willing to work and he was willing to fight. That was why they had chosen him. Those who had ignored their counsel—and ignored Kilaun's—and remained behind were gone, dead, buried. They spoke to no one.

Kilaun had been chosen and had unhesitatingly accepted the guidance he'd been provided. It had not led him astray.

It had been helpful having Chu with him on the journey west, but maybe it wasn't worth it. Chu was good at things that required brute strength. He never seemed to aspire to anything more than helping. Perhaps whatever went on at The Pass had done away with that version of Chu, or perhaps Kilaun had misunderstood his brother all along.

Their journey west had taken nearly a year. They left the day that winter started to turn into spring. For the first month, they had to keep moving from when they woke up until when they nestled up against one another to sleep. If they didn't keep moving, they would freeze.

For the first part of the trip, they had food they carried with them. Dried meats, flatbread, canned food, candy bars, whatever they could get a hold of before they left.

When the food ran out, they took to hunting. Kilaun was best at foraging and Chu took care of the trapping. It was on this trip that Chu learned to trap. He became a master. Focusing on such a small task was comforting for his small mind. Of course, they had learned to trap as children, but that was when they didn't need to.

Meanwhile, Kilaun learned everything that could be eaten in the wild. Humans had become completely separate from the wilderness. The ancestors gave Kilaun gifts on his journey – berries in any season, mushrooms that told him whether they were edible, roots that smelled sweetly and boiled up well. The men were somehow able to get enough to eat to sustain them on their long journey.

They had intentionally kept away from the towns and cities, clinging to the woods and the rivers and the wild. Those were their friends. It seemed as though violence and death was the new way of man, and Kilaun wanted no part of it. Guided by nature and those that had come before him, he would survive in his own way.

It had been a dream that had told Kilaun to go west. A dream with a special quality, not just any dream. Some were different. Like the one from last night. Kilaun closed his eyes and guided his mind to the world of that dream.

His town. The town empty. Abandoned? Yet, it remained alive. The continuum. Kilaun had come to understand that even without the townspeople, the town would be alive. It existed outside of them and outside of him. It grew strong, tall grass without them all. It had its own life force.

The pathway. He walked the pathway of the small stones. The stones were placed there. The stones were order. The stones represented the things we make in our lives. The steps through the wild that we can't control. The steps were Kilaun's contribution to the world. The steps grew fewer and farther apart. Yes, this felt correct. Kilaun's contribution had been diminishing. He had been coasting and was now paying the price, losing control, slipping.

The porch. It had looked like wood but had been something else entirely. Watch your step? He discarded this idea as too simple, too literal. Appearances can be deceiving, certainly. Perhaps this was the message the false porch was meant to convey. He pushed this idea around in his head, not yet satisfied. Of course the porch was wood, it was always wood, it was never something he'd have thought about or looked twice at. Perhaps other assumptions were false as well, perhaps things he took for granted needed to be reevaluated. Yes. Vigilance and close observation. The floor, the porch, the building materials of his home. It seemed to Kilaun that the people were the material of the village. Was he being warned about hidden agendas? Perhaps Kilaun had been too trusting, had tried too hard to find the good in people.

The room. Why was he in the guest room? He might take from it that he was no longer master of his house, of the village. And also, the guest room was now where his brother stayed. Were the ancestors drawing Kilaun's attention to his brother? The dream was serving as a warning.

They had never been in the same space. Kilaun in one, Chu in another. Kilaun resented Chu. Things were easy for him; it was easy being simple. Now, here he was, entertaining Kilaun's wife, entertaining the townspeople, entertaining even the ornery cook. He was a damned fool, the town simpleton, and the punch line of every joke you could come up with. And, yet, he stood in front of all with no fear on the night of the assembly and defied his brother. New to the town, knowing nothing about what they had been through for the past five years, defying him, deciding what was best. Chu had been in the Pass. He had accomplished nothing and yet he now saw fit to take the reins from Kilaun who had created safety from cold wilderness and community from strangers.

Kilaun had been lying on the bed. He understood that he was being told he had been complacent. And his complacence, lying prone, made him vulnerable, there in Chu's room. Vulnerable in Chu's space. Something with the ceiling? He wasn't sure. But the world started changing. It wasn't his anymore. The town, via its own will – It came for him.

His cuts. The grass had cut him, the bushes had devoured him. Something growing, something he couldn't control. Had the cuts come from the path Chu had walked with the Outsider woman in his arms, with the people, Kilaun's people, failing to stop him?

In the end, all his blood had been shed for these ungrateful people. The vines, which he now viewed as representing the town, came for him and devoured his life force, leaving him empty. He knew terror in that dream like he had never felt the equal of in life. He had been paralyzed by his fear.

Kilaun could see that he'd allowed his emotions, perhaps some fear, but more often sadness and anger, to paralyze him, that he'd allowed himself the luxury of indecision because of self-pity. Kilaun did not cope well with powerlessness. He never had. He had a flash of a moment when he was a child and was beaten by another boy. That afternoon, he crushed a rabbit's skull in his hand. The eyeball popped out of the head and hung from a tendon outside of Kilaun's tiny clenched fist. He pushed the savage thought out of his mind. He was only a child then.

The mushrooms, though. What were those? He had foraged mushrooms on the trip with his brother. Even after, when the summers were wet. Still with his brother, though. The food that nourished his brother growing out of Kilaun in the dream. Kilaun gave so much to Chu and now Chu wanted even more. Chu wanted his wife and he wanted his town.

Kilaun's anger had mounted.

He had these images, the vines and the blood and the grass and the false wood, and he thought of his brother. His brother carrying that corpse across the square. His brother touching his wife. His brother standing so much taller than him. His brother going into the maid's house in secret followed by the townspeople. He had seen it with his own eyes. And Kilaun, laying there in the bed, paralyzed, drunk dry by the town that he had breathed life into. His brother, his own brother was the driving force behind it all. The force that pushed Kilaun toward his own death.

Kilaun now knew that the ancestors had given him this dream as a warning. They were warning him that his brother would keep pushing. And that, if Kilaun did not stop him, he would eventually push too far.

37

Qaniit rode furiously along the frozen river toward the Pass. The rhythm of Buck's hooves breaking through the snow, the biting cold on her skin—for the time being, her world was reduced to the immediate and the tangible. The powerful animal beneath her. The tundra stretching endlessly before them. The rhythmic drum of hooves pounding through snow. Bitter cold, stinging her face. This was what life was meant to feel like.

She rode up the river and into the gulch, exploring up the creek toward the old mine. She gave the horse rest at a spot of melt. Qaniit kicked around and looked at the trees. Just a couple miles from the village and each tree was so foreign, with their own little lives that she knew nothing about. Even the bark on the white spruces weathered differently out this way. It felt so good to find something fascinating again. Fascination seemed like just one of a number of feelings that had been closed off to her for years.

Qaniit made her way back to town exhausted and happy. Buck's mane was crusted in frozen sweat and snow and she was ready to cool him off and warm herself up. She trotted toward town feeling as though her life was worth living, as though there were possibilities for her once again. She hopped off at the edge of the village and walked Buck in on the back road. Raised voices in the square attracted her attention. The Qaniit of several days ago might have just chosen to ignore it and go on about her business. This Qaniit would not do this.

An argument. Two men shouting against a backdrop of chattering bystanders. She hoped it was not Kilaun. She liked liking him again. She approached, reluctantly.

But no, it wasn't Kilaun. She could tell Chena's son from his shape, but not the other one.

She moved in closer and saw a familiar face.

"Leif!" she exclaimed, walking Buck over by the crude reins of rope.

Leif left Soapy there looking fairly terrified, and came straight over. He put his arm around Buck and patted his shoulder, whispering in his ear words of comfort.

"What's going on?" Qaniit asked.

"The cook's boy's the one who stole him." Leif cast an aggressive glare in the direction of his diminutive adversary. Soapy had already been backing away while the older man's eyes were elsewhere.

Leif reached for the reins that Qaniit held. She pulled them away from him.

"Stole?" Qaniit did not comprehend.

"That's right." He snatched the reins and pressed his body up against Buck's. He'd spoken more words to this horse in the last few years than he had to any human.

Qaniit could only stammer as her mind fought against Leif's words, "But – a trade?"

"I declined his offer to trade. Why would I give up Buck?" He looked with affection at the horse that stood there impassively.

"I thought—I thought maybe—you wanted me to have him."

Leif turned his eyes from the horse to the woman.

"He—did he steal Buck for—you?" Leif asked.

"He gave me Buck. As a gift. But I didn't know—." She couldn't bring herself to say that the horse was stolen. This would be an admission that Buck was not hers. This would mean never experiencing the euphoria of just a few minutes ago again.

"I had no idea he gave Buck to you."

"Leif, please. Let's put Buck up and go inside."

He affixed his eyes to hers and paused to let her know that he was serious. "I would sooner butcher this horse right here than enter your husband's house."

It was ludicrous, of course, as he'd never do such a thing, but men and their pride were not subject to reason and she hadn't meant to go to the house she shared with Kilaun anyhow. "Tali's. Let's go to Tali's. She would be glad to see you, I'm sure."

"All right then. But if it's just the same to you, I'd like to keep Buck nearby." Leif made no mention of his previous encounter with the woman who was once a girl he knew.

Qaniit grimaced. "Are you worried about someone stealing him? Where would they take him, back to your house?"

Under layers of grime and hair, Leif flushed, unused to company or teasing or having his horse stolen. He said nothing but didn't move. Qaniit sighed. "We'll keep him close." She remembered his well enough to know from his silence that he wouldn't have budged without the concession.

His expression softened ever so slightly. The two walked over to the small barn, left from back when the village had horses.

Qaniit put the horse up and made him comfortable. She put him in the stall near the wood stove, and tended the small fire going in it to keep him warm. She quickly fetched him some parsnips from the nearby root cellar. Leif watched her care for him.

When they arrived at Tali's, Tali and Libby went in the back room to give them some privacy.

Qaniit and Leif sat at the only table in the room and looked at one another. "So this is what we need to do to get you to come into town?" she asked, straight faced.

He chuckled and relaxed. "I'm sorry, Qaniit."

"For what? I'm the one that stole your horse."

"Aw, hell, I'd have given you the horse."

Qaniit looked down at her dirty nails.

"Shit, Qaniit. Take him. It's OK."

Tears welled in her eyes. The horse had now been given to her twice. But she couldn't accept it this time. Her husband had ruined it. Ruined everything. Brought her feelings for him back from the dead just to butcher them more thoroughly.

"Leif, I can't. You know I can't." God damn her husband.

"Shadow had her foal and he'll be a strong one. Maybe in a year if Shadow is up for it we can get her and Buck together again."

"Leif.... No. Really." But her voice lacked resolve. She couldn't turn down the horse.

"I know you always loved them. I'd give you Shadow if I could but she's a momma now. And I don't need that many mouths to feed anyway."

Leif had always been generous with her. From the first time he found her, huddled behind a broken down gaming table on the ship with Noah, he had been nothing but kind. And he never wanted a thing from her.

"Oh, Leif. I shouldn't, but I can't say no. He'll be all I have to live for here." She spoke in a whisper, conscious that there were others in the house.

"Take him and take good care of him. For me."

Qaniit sniffed and held back tears. "All right, Leif. If this is what I can do to pay you back for all your kindness," she joked. "But now, we're even."

He laughed. "I reckon we are."

*

Qaniit saw Leif off and he went home on foot, the way he came. Tali had gone over to the main house to put together some food to take with him. The little bit that they could give him would never have paid him back for his gift.

She watched him until he was nearly out of sight because it felt like her duty given that she owed him so much and saw him so rarely. But, before he was twenty yards off, Qaniit's thoughts had turned to her husband. How he could possibly steal from Leif, lie to her, and involve Chena's son in the whole thing? Qaniit could not possibly understand. He had been reclusive. Paranoid. Qaniit thought that he might well be going out of his mind. It was not the first time she had wondered. She'd always been more skeptical of his talk about "the Ancestors" than most. But that had seemed harmless. This, this behavior was something entirely different – dishonorable.

She didn't say anything to him that day when he got home from the ridge. He seemed to still be in love with her again and he tried to be affectionate. She just turned her face and went back to her drawing. She didn't want to tell him that she knew about Leif. Part of her wanted to see if he would ever come clean. The other part knew that he was already too far gone toward ruined.

38

Libby awakened to find the world just as dark as it was when she'd gone to bed. It seemed as though "day" this far north was a name arbitrarily granted with no basis in reality. What Libby thought of as "day" included sun. She pictured chirping birds, flowers and greenery for good measure.

Here, you were lucky to get a few hours of twilight. And if it were cloudy? The day was barely even worth noticing. But it wasn't as though the winter-weak sun had the power to warm a person anyhow.

Regular food and warmth had cheered Libby initially but, as her life settled into a routine, she found herself feeling no more joy than she had when held captive. Not that she wished to return to that state, but then the hunger had dulled her emotions so much that her misery now felt that much sharper.

It had also now dawned on her that she would forever be an "Outsider" here. Her friends would be few. Suspicion would be the default attitude toward her. At first, she thought she could get past it but, as the novelty of her nominal freedom wore off, she found bitterness toward the townspeople growing within her. They had just gone on about their business while Libby, having done nothing, remained locked up and hungry, for months. They wouldn't have treated a dog that way. People might kill each other on the mainland but better to kill someone than just leave them to die.

If it hadn't been for the giant brother of the boss of this dump, had she'd have died there. He had his own moral compass. Unlike the rest of them, he wasn't afraid to read it. Maybe if you're that big you aren't scared of anything.

Because one had to do something, Libby walked every day. The walks weren't pleasant because they were cold and anyone she encountered only served to remind her of what an outcast she was, but they were a distraction and they helped pass the time. She often fantasized about being somewhere else. The scenery changed. Sometimes she thought that being back home would be better, but the gulf between here and there was wider than just the distance between the two places.

This was a warm day, which meant that it might pass zero. Tali didn't have a thermometer but the cook did and sometimes Tali would come back and report on how warm or cold it had been that day. Libby was sure this was the warmest she'd seen it in the month since the big man took her out of the jail.

Libby usually just walked around town, or a little up the old road. Even if the cold hadn't kept her from going to far, her fear of the wolves would have. She had seen them herself, including the big one a few times. He looked to be two hundred pounds. Bigger than she knew they came. And she didn't want to get caught alone by him and a few friends.

She was walking the back road, down by the spring, when the small man approached. Tali had mentioned him to her, so Libby knew he was the cook's son, but she hadn't spoken much to him.

"Hello!" he said, more loudly than necessary.

Libby didn't really like anyone right now, but she could tell that she especially didn't like this man.

The man cleared snow off a rock and gestured for Libby to sit down.

"I'm all right," she replied.

"You must be Libby." Without waiting for a response, he continued, "I'm Soapy."

The occasional word or sound from Libby was all that was necessary to keep the little man talking for several minutes. At first, it was entirely idle, mindless chatter, and she was cold and disinterested. He paused for a moment but, just as Libby was ready to excuse herself, he found he had more to say.

"I bet you wish you could get out of here."

This gave Libby pause. Where was he going with this? She said nothing.

The cadence of his speech changed. He wasn't just filling up space with words anymore. He wanted something.

He leaned in toward her conspiratorially. "I could get you out of here, you know."

Libby was intrigued but didn't trust him. She opted for a noncommittal response. This was a known crony of Kilaun. "Where would I want to go? It's nice here." Her mouth could form the words but her eyes made plain that they were false. Soapy noticed.

The little man snorted. "Ha! Nice here." There was genuine disdain in his voice. Libby found it heartening. Perhaps he was sincere after all.

"I imagine you would want to go pretty much anywhere else. I, myself, am going to the mainland."

Libby looked at him. All these people had told her that she couldn't get to the mainland this time of year and she could imagine what attempting the journey would be like. She was inclined to think that Soapy was a liar, a cheat, a fool, or some combination of the three.

"Oh, you don't think so, eh?" He sounded disappointed in her. "Maybe you think I don't seem like the type to pull it off."

He glanced about and leaned in closer. "Well, I've got a secret," he whispered.

The words and his manner reminded her of a small child and yet she found herself intrigued nonetheless.

"All these people can't get down there right now. You can't walk across the glacier this time of year. Too cold, no supplies, can't get across fast enough. But I happen to have access to a horse."

"The horse you stole from the old man?" Libby asked.

Soapy got huffy, "Don't believe everything you hear. Now I was hired by Kilaun to trade the old man for the horse because exchange is what I do. The old man was difficult from the start and I guess he had regrets after the deal. That's not my fault. The horse is still here, right? Think he'd just walk off an' leave it if I stole it? The old man got everything the horse was worth."

Libby had been able to make out the tone and some of the words of the conversation Qaniit and Leif shared. She did not believe this man. "So what did you get?" Libby asked, critically.

"That's my own business, darlin'. I know how to make my living." False bravado. What a vile little creature.

"Uh huh." Libby started to meander a bit. Soapy followed.

"Well, that's fine. You don't have to say anything now, but you just think on it. Nobody else can get you out of here. You find me."

Libby thought about it. She really did want to get out. Even if she had to go with this greasy little man to do it, she would. She thought about whether she trusted him to get her back to the Port, and decided that she didn't trust him for anything. But she trusted her wits and if she had to get away from him she could. She didn't even think he could take her in a fight.

"What about food?" she asked.

He stood closer to her. "Honey, there's food everywhere. At least for me. I'm the best trapper and hunter in this town. Don't worry, you won't go hungry." He looked her up and down, staring at her breasts despite her bulky coat. God, he was disgusting.

"All right, mister, what is it you want from me then? What's this going to cost me?"

"Wonderful!" he said. "You won't regret it, you –"

"So what's the charge?" she interrupted.

"Charge?"

"You said you know how to make a living, right? So what are you thinking you're going to get out of this? You don't offer your guide services for free, do you? If they were any good I don't think you would…" Libby feigned concern. She'd rather pay than have this twerp think he could crawl in her bed for payment. The thought of going to bed with him made her shudder.

"Of course there's a charge!" he quickly piped up. "I'll figure out the charge and let you know when we're leaving," Soapy said. "It will be in the next week or two."

"Fine." Libby said, and she walked off. She didn't half believe him that he would leave here in the middle of winter and she didn't half believe that she would go with him. But if keeping him on the hook left her the option should he actually get it together and go, then it was worth it.

She hoped she didn't have to see him in the meanwhile. Just standing near him made her feel like she needed a bath.

39

Qaniit had made it through the evening with her husband by simply detaching. It was no different than she had been, except that he didn't hide in the office to avoid her. He had, of course, asked her how she was enjoying the horse and seemed quite proud of himself. She fell asleep on the couch and tried to pretend it was an accident. She really had limited material.

The following day, she took a ride up the ridge. It was a little dodgy in places but when necessary she would hop off and walk Buck up. He was such a majestic creature. She still couldn't believe she had him now.

She was well up the side of the ridge when she saw the abandoned miner's cabin. She hadn't been inside in years. Buck tramped right up the old trail without any hesitation.

The old cabin was still intact. The white spruce logs had grayed, but the roof looked strong. She though how nice it would have been to live that high up, with views of the valley below. She tied Buck up and stood on the porch. She could even see their tiny village a couple miles off. It looked so insignificant from all the way up there.

The idea of going inside awakened some nostalgia within her. The place was a reminder that, despite the seemingly endless sameness of her current existence, life was not fixed.

The old door creaked open without any trouble. It was a single, open room, with one window on each wall. In the middle of the room was an old wood stove. There were books lining an entire wall. She wondered what kind of man had lived there.

Qaniit looked at the wall of books and dragged her fingers along the bindings. There were many that she hadn't read in years, if at all. She had read regularly when she'd lived on the mainland but lately it seemed as though she'd lost the taste for it. The world within most of them had little more to offer her than children's fairy tales. The lives and concerns of the characters had nothing to do with Qaniit.

There was a pile of wood next to the stove. On a whim, Qaniit decided to start fire. She wondered how long it had been since this fireplace had been used. The wood had been sitting there for a long time. It was dry and caught quickly.

She settled into a chair and flipped through a book of poetry. She started melting a pot of snow for the horse, who was entertaining himself outside by chewing on some alder. She felt at peace and alone, as though she'd found a spot in the world for herself.

The book of poetry remained open in her lap but she was staring out the window.

Her trance was broken by a voice from outside. She knew to be caught alone could be dangerous, but when she opened the door she saw that it was only Chu, happily petting Buck. The big man wore an shameless grin that seemed to belong more to a toddler than to a buffalo of a man. She called out a greeting and he turned to wave at her like a child. She smiled. "Hello, Chu."

"I was checking my traps," he said, holding up a few furry carcasses. "I saw your fire. Are you okay?"

"Oh, I'm fine. Just exploring. Do you want to come in?"

*

Chu was an enigma to her. He was childlike in so many ways, still filled with wonder by things other adults had ceased to find interesting like seashells or bird's nests. Yet when the other adults cowered and did whatever was expedient, Chu was the only one who'd even considered what was right.

He looked at her and smiled. He was being kind of silly, nonthreatening. Kilaun was always so serious. Kilaun's main objective was always to show how very serious he was. Qaniit didn't find that as attractive as playfulness.

Kilaun had never been playful, really. There was certainly a time that he was not angry and unbearable. She reached back into her memory to try and find the man she had married. She had seen it earlier today in one of his manic episodes, but it was just another act, a tool of manipulation. He had increasingly been resorting to such devices as he lost his purity of intent.

Qaniit sat next to Chu on the dusty couch. They stared out the window together and she realized it was as comfortable as it had been before he arrived. She'd treasured the solitude then, but she didn't resent the intrusion. Not by Chu.

Chu said nothing to disturb Qaniit's moment, lost in her inner world. It was his simplicity, she thought, that allowed the moment to be all it was. It was so quiet and white and perfect.

She was dimly aware, although lost in her reverie, that she would soon have to go back to her real life and her husband. But, for this moment, she was who she was in this space, and as Chu watched her tend the stove that afternoon, she liked who it was that he saw. She was just a person again, just a woman tending the stove. His brother's wife at that. She missed being just a person, just a woman, as opposed to being someone to manipulate, ensnare, conquer and control. That's how Kilaun saw her, she thought.

No outside observer would have claimed that Qaniit did or felt anything improper that day. Qaniit felt as though she were living in the unreal world of literature that she'd long ago discarded. A temporary stay in an alien land might have its uses after all.

When the sun started to set in the afternoon, Qaniit and Chu both left the cabin. Like a story that sticks with you, that day became part of her, her perfect day. And Chu, Chu was perfect too. While she thought perhaps it was crueler to experience a few hours of the life she might've wanted than to never know it at all, the recollection made her happy, not wistful. She thought that perhaps one of those old novels would've said that she left her heart there, in the old miner's cabin. But the rest of her went back down the mountain, with Chu, to face their respective destinies.

40

A small woman, or a child, dwarf-like and malformed, in a dark attic with a light shining in her face. She squinted and twitched from the strain. She moved closer, horrified, and backed away, quickly. Her movements were punctuated like an insect's. She came close and tore her shirt away, revealing her bare chest, which had only a thin layer of papery skin protecting a wildly beating heart.

She pressed her malformed face up close to Kilaun. He could see her heart through the thin piece of skin, not even flesh, just beating away. She became fearful. The more fearful she became, the harder the heart beat. It beat fast and faster, harder and harder, showing itself from behind the nearly translucent film of skin. She was a repulsive, hideous creature.

Meanwhile, an elegant woman sat in a restaurant with high ceilings and red curtains at a table with many gentlemen. There were fine foods on the table and shiny silverware, but only spoons. Spoons of all different sizes and shapes and metals.

She was clearly rich and sophisticated, clever and entertaining, and every so often she would say something that would cause the entire table to erupt in laughter. The men leaned forward with uncontained amusement, using their napkins to shield them from her apparently striking wit. The woman was magnificent to behold, with freckled skin hanging on her shoulders like a shawl. Each of the men looked up to her and respected her. Each of them loved her and served her.

The lights in the room dimmed and all heads turned to the stage. The elegant woman cocked her head, examining a young woman who appeared from behind the curtains. The men looked at each other and nodded. The elegant woman stood, as if to give the signal to the men that she approved. The young woman looked just enough like her. Just enough.

The elegant woman and her men went to get the girl but the woman was somehow pulled into a side room without her admirers noticing. The men continued toward the young woman on the stage.

The magnificent woman, having been pulled aside, was engaged in an argument with a man. Their words weren't comprehensible, but both grew more and more agitated until the confrontation became physical, wrestling and hitting one another, eventually falling to the floor. As the fight continued, the woman's clothes were removed until she was entirely naked, rolling on the floor, fighting this man.

Somehow, she overcame him. She rose to her feet, her clothes inexplicably returning to their assigned places, as perfectly arranged as before. Kilaun became aware that the girl from the stage was screaming. The woman seemed to understand what this meant and she raced to find the girl that looked like her. Just enough like her. Nobody had run to help the woman, but she was there to help the girl. But she was too late when she got there and the girl she saw was gone. The men stood there, licking their lips and patting their bellies, full of the meaty roast of woman they just devoured.

A knife. A knife was cutting a human from the top of its head to its genitals. A skinning cut. Hands peeled back the human's outside and ripped it from its muscles and organs. A trousered knee pressed down on one flapping side of the skin for leverage to pull against the other flapping side. Through tugging and pulling, the wrapping was torn off its fleshy package. Getting down to what the human was underneath the skin, but it was only flesh and that is all. But that is something too.

And these were the things that Kilaun saw when he was sleeping. These things and more. And these became the things he thought about when he was awake.

41

The week after seeing Qaniit at the miner's cabin, Chu thought a lot about her. He tried not to, but it was no use. He thought about her small, pretty hands and her hair. And her laugh. He would be carrying water or checking his traps or chopping wood and suddenly realize he'd been thinking about her for half an hour.

Chu knew she was his brother's wife and that he would not want his brother to suffer losing her, so it never occurred to him to try and take Qaniit for his own. But, still, he daydreamed, wondering what kinds of things she liked other than horses. He would think about nice things he might do for her, then shake his head about how silly that was, and how she did not want to have anything to do with him in that way. He would tell himself he'd be better off focusing his thoughts on somebody else. But there was nobody else and, even if there was, he would have still thought of Qaniit.

The woman Chu had before, years ago, was also kind. He had left her behind when he came west with his brother. She did not want him to go and she would not go with him. But Chu felt it was his place to go with his brother on the long journey and to protect him and feed him. The ancestors did not speak to Chu the way they did to his brother and Chu respected his brother for having been chosen.

Kilaun had done a lot to build up the town and he had sacrificed a lot to come west and follow the ancestors' plan. It was a noble, honorable thing that Kilaun did and Chu knew that. By Chu's way of thinking, his brother deserved Qaniit. He had earned her.

But his brother had not been so noble and honorable lately and, even if he deserved Qaniit, she didn't deserve to be married to someone behaving the way Kilaun had been. He had been increasingly short tempered and barely spoke to anybody. He had given Qaniit the horse but it didn't seem they were getting along any better. Chu was slow, but he was not stupid, and he was sure his brother gave Qaniit the horse to try to make her happy. Chu did not have anything so fancy as a horse to give her. But he pushed that thought out of his mind like the others as one he should not be having.

Still, the thoughts came to him. And Qaniit was never far from his mind.

Chu was in the shed when the thought crept back in. He picked up a block of wood lying on the floor and began to whittle away at it. He sat on a bucket, backside and fingers cold, for the next hour, whittling away. When he was done, he looked down in his hands and saw a small, carved horse.

42

Soapy hobbled along. His damned foot hadn't recovered since the last time he went out to the old man's house. He had sacrificed the better part of a toe, and for what? Nothing. So Kilaun's snotty wife could have a horse. What'd he get? Nothing. No meat, no salt, no tobacco, no trinkets. He had tried to talk to Kilaun about it, but the man was vacant, useless.

This town is about to go to shit.

If it doesn't have a leader, if the leader is just a sack of flesh, absent and shell-like, then it will be like the other towns, which aren't towns at all. Just people living near each other, wild-like, needing only a little excuse to cheat or kill one another.

Soapy pictured the devolution of his village and wondered if Tali would take to whoring. That's what women did when times got rough, right? Then she couldn't turn up her nose at him. He liked the thought.

He figured he could get by in a world like that – he was all right with grifting and the like. While he never begrudged a man a good grift, he knew it was better if it wasn't against someone who knows when you are home, not home, cutting wood, in the outhouse, or when your wife is at home or in the outhouse. Better to cheat someone who you'll never see again. Well, unless you go to try and trade them for a horse and they won't cooperate. Can't avoid situations like that.

*

Again, Soapy walked at night, but this time it'd be worth it. He felt no guilt about going after the old man's other horse and his anger kept the fear he'd felt last time away. He couldn't believe what the old man had done. Humiliated him in town! It was inconceivable. *A man doesn't do that to another man.* Soapy was doing a job, that was it. If the old man had a problem with it, he should have gone to Kilaun.

That was a week ago and still Kilaun's wife had been prancing around on that horse like she was some storybook queen. Soapy wondered what she traded the old man to keep the horse. She wasn't the most innocent type, really. His mother kept going on about what a hussy she was, running around with Kilaun's brother. And now the old man! Soapy couldn't believe that Kilaun fussed over that kind of a woman. That kind of woman needed to be put in her place. Smack her around a little and she'd step into line in a hurry.

Now, the maid on the other hand, she was worth a fuss. But she'd been giving Soapy the cold shoulder. He wasn't getting anywhere with her. She'd just been holed up in her cabin for the better part of the winter since the Outsider started living there. Soapy'd gone by a few times but she just sent him straight away. She was turning snotty like Kilaun's wife, really.

The Outsider was a new development. Soapy hadn't thought much of her, but a woman was a woman, and she wasn't bad to look at. Finally getting a little meat on her, too, so you could tell she was a woman instead of just a sack of bones. He wondered how old she was. Older than him he was sure, but at least he probably couldn't get her pregnant. Last thing he needed was a baby on the way just as he broke free of that crappy little village.

Soapy got to Leif's stable at about the same time as before, the cold, crystal clear middle of the night. Stars above and the moonlight showing him the way. This time he was doing his own job, though. With a horse and a pony they'd have no trouble crossing the glacier, even in winter. The Outsider would do just fine tagging along with Soapy. Maybe he could even get a reward for bringing her back to the mainland. Maybe even get set up with a job.

Soapy was careful this time, quiet as a mouse. He stepped one step at a time, one step a minute, careful not to wake the old man. He got over to the stables and opened the door just as carefully. Slowly, quietly, intently. He got the door open without a sound. He was nearly home free.

He crept inside and saw the horses in the stall. The mare was a good lookin' horse, could haul a lot of gear or carry Soapy if need be. Not that he was a heavy man. She gave a little snort, but it wasn't too loud. "Shhh…" Soapy soothed her as he approached.

In the middle of his third "Shhh…" and five more steps to the stall, Soapy took a step that didn't connect with the ground and he fell clear through the floor. Bewildered and stunned, he looked up to see that he was a floor lower than he'd started, and in a big, dirt box at that. His leg hurt something awful. He fought the urge to cry out in pain.

He had to get out of there.

But there was no getting out of there to be had. Hopping onto his good leg, Soapy tried scrambling up the dirt walls, but there wasn't anything to get a hold of, and it was too cold to take his gloves off. There was nothing he could pile up to get out. Just a meager bale of hay, which barely got him any higher.

He looked for a rope, anything, so maybe he could pull himself out. But, again, the walls were a good eight feet tall and Soapy wasn't close to that. He was legitimately screwed.

He unpacked the hay bale and made a nest for himself. He had bundled up more this time so he figured he'd be fine. He wished he hadn't left the door to the stable open, as all the heat would go right out the opening, but he couldn't very well have anticipated this. He didn't know whether the floor had given way or what, it had happened so fast.

Soapy was so angry that the old man had left his stable in such a state of disrepair that something like this could happen to him. As he curled up into the scratchy hay, with his throbbing leg outstretched, he thought about what the old man would need to do to make it up to him if he broke his damn leg. He reckoned he'd know by morning just how screwed he really was.

43

Chena woke up in the morning to find her boy gone. Again. That goddamn boy that wasn't worth the old boots he wore. Did he not appreciate her? Did he not realize that it gave her trouble to have him out doing lord only knows what in the middle of the night? Chena swore that she wasn't going to put up with this nonsense much longer. The last time Soapy'd been out all night he came back with frostbite and lost half a toe. He was still limping around from that and now here he was gone again. She was sure Kilaun'd put him up to something.

She threw some logs on the fire but didn't even fix breakfast before she put on her boots and went looking for Kilaun. He may have been the boss of her when she was working but he sure wasn't boss enough to be sending her boy out into the night losing body parts and whatnot.

Chena marched out of the house and headed over to Kilaun's, but stopped just before she let herself in the back door. Qaniit and Chu were sitting in the kitchen, each on either side of the counter, talking to one another.

Chena watched them through the window and she saw the way they spoke and looked at one another. She had known there was trouble before, but seeing the way Qaniit leaned over toward him, her fingers dancing on the sides of a mug, made everything clear. Chu sat there, mumbling shyly, and Qaniit threw her head back laughing, reaching across and touching his arm with affection.

If Chena had any doubts about her suspicions, she didn't any more. Oh, yes, this was trouble.

Her son forgotten, Chena reveled in the perceived misdeeds of the high and mighty. Qaniit, above everyone else, even her husband. Chu, the insolent buffoon. Even Kilaun, so important and serious and look what was happening behind his back!

Such knowledge! Such power!

There was now no question in the old woman's mind that something indecent was going on between Kilaun's wife and his brother. They were up to no good at all.

A knowing smile on her face, Chena pushed her way through the door and sauntered up to the pair. She looked down her nose at them, haughty, knowing.

Qaniit at first furrowed her brow, trying to look confused, but she then stood up and folded her arms. "Is something amiss, Chena?"

"Why, yes, dear, I think that something is."

Qaniit continued to play dumb. "Why don't you enlighten us then, *dear*."

Chena looked back and forth between them, her cruel grin feeding off the discomfort in the room. Her eyes strayed down to Chu's crotch and very evenly traced a perfect straight line over to Qaniit's. Her meaning was quite clear.

"Chena!" Qaniit gasped. "There is *nothing* to be concerned about. And, even if there was, it wouldn't be any of *your* concern. Understand?"

Qaniit really was a snotty one and she was stupid indeed if she thought that Chena was going to forget what she just saw. No, thank you. Chena did not have any desire to be part of that kind of drama and so long as she worked here she would not lie about a god damned thing that she knew or saw, whether it would get Qaniit's head chopped off or not.

"I hear ya," Chena said, turning to Chu, who had a stupid, prey-like expression on his face. But she came over here for a reason, not just to watch Qaniit and Chu play house behind Kilaun's back. So she asked, "Where's Soapy?"

Qaniit raised her eyebrows. "No idea."

"Your no-good husband send him out on another 'errand'? Maybe he decided you needed an elephant this time?"

Qaniit scowled and stiffened. And now Chena knew that Qaniit knew the horse was stolen. Chena hadn't been sure.

"Kilaun's up on the ridge. If you want to ask him, you can hike up there yourself."

"I'll pass, but you tell him my boy better come home this time with all his toes and fingers."

"If you want me to say that to him, I will certainly do so," Qaniit said smugly.

Chena scowled. She knew well that Qaniit did not talk to her husband enough to pass along any such message.

Chena strode back to the door. She paused before stepping through it and, while cold air rushed in through the open door, the old woman's scowl reshaped itself into a smile that would have given the devil himself pause.

44

Leif's morning started like any other. At this point in the winter, his routine had become a part of him and he automatically moved from station to station entirely engaged in whatever he was doing in that moment, be it enjoying a cup of tea or chopping wood.

It was not until he went out to see the horses that he realized this day was not going to be just like the one before it. He saw as soon as he rounded the corner of the cabin that the door to the barn was ajar. Being the creature of routine that he was, he knew things were not as he'd left them.

He paused and sighed deeply, hoping he was prepared for whatever was to come. The principal emotion was disappointment, a wistfulness that his routine had been interrupted. Winter life could be oppressive, but it allowed Leif a measure of peace that he did not relish passing.

But he wasted no time contemplating the possibilities that might have led to the door being unfastened this morning. Wistfulness and regret would be of no use to him in confronting whatever awaited him today, and so he dismissed the intruding emotions.

He strode back to the cabin door in a quiet, measured manner, and when he next passed the spot where he'd first spied the open door his expression was the same as it had been when he'd passed this spot the day before, and the day before that, and the day before that. Although, this time, he held an axe with both hands.

When he reached the open door and looked in, there were Shadow and her foal. And a hole in the floor.

He crept toward the hole slowly and silently and peered over the edge. A mass of fur and clothing was huddled in the corner. Leif somehow recognized the mass and sighed as he stepped back.

"Hey!" came a voice from the cellar. "Hey, I heard you! I'm down here! Let me out! Help!"

Leif moved back to the hole and looked inside. Yes, it was Kilaun's loathsome little thief.

"Hey! Let me out, I'm freezing! Please! Hey!"

"What in the hell are you doin' down there?"

"Your floor broke! I coulda been killed! Come on, get me out! I'm freezing!" The thief huffed into his hands, though he'd probably been unable to feel them for quite some time.

This response did not please the old man. He adopted a businesslike expression and retreated from the would-be thief's sight for a moment. When he returned he was carrying something large. A board. He placed the board over the hole in the floor and all became dark.

Leif calmly walked across the now-covered hole as a stream of obscenity-laced gibberish spewed forth from within it.

While Leif fed Shadow and the foal he heard begging and threatening and cajoling and imploring words emerging from the hole, though all were slightly muffled by the covering he'd placed above it.

Leif was satisfied that the little man was no threat from down there, so while he was out of earshot caring for the chickens, he fully engaged the chore, his mind settling back into his routine. When he returned, the racket had died down.

He opened the hole back up. The little man had not learned the intended lesson from his extended stay down there. As soon as the he heard the scraping of the board being removed above him, he started up. "My damn leg's broke! You can't leave me down here! You're messing with the wrong—." The board fell back in place as his prisoner finished his shouted sentence.

The old man walked impassively back to the cabin, paying no mind to the shouts that faded as he went. He returned a short time later, though in no hurry, with an armload of wood. If his guest would be staying for the day, he would need a fire in order to not freeze to death, so Leif made one in the barrel stove in the stable.

There were chores to be done. Winter would not take a day off so neither would Leif. He chopped and hauled and fixed in the necessary amounts, paying little mind to his company. To the extent that he thought of anything other than the task he was at any given moment accomplishing, it was his last break in routine his mind turned to, his trip to town.

He felt close to Qaniit, seeing her again, and it made him feel more human. But what he couldn't really get over was seeing Tali, Tali, no longer a child, but a woman. It occurred to him that it should make him feel old, but what it really made him feel was good, part of something.

The town had looked almost the same. A few of the older buildings were gone. Probably taken apart for firewood in the cold snap last winter. That had been a rough one.

After lunch, Leif went back out to the stable to find it quiet. He pulled back the board. The man beneath it had run out of threats and promises.

"Please, mister. I'm so cold. An' I'm hurt bad. Please let me out, mister." His speech slurred, as though his face was numb.

"Well, if I let you out, how do I know you ain't gonna run off with my horse?"

"I think my leg's broke. I dunno if I can stand. But I won't do nothin'. You win. Just please, please let me be warm again."

Leif felt his point has been made, and so he dropped down the ladder. When Soapy reached the top he stretched a hand out toward the older man. Leif stared blankly and remained motionless. Clearly, the little thief did not understand the nature of their relationship.

Soapy grumbled about his leg, but Leif could see that he was able to put some weight on it. It wasn't broken.

"Unless your Daddy's out here somewhere I don't think anybody's gonna carry you."

Leif and Soapy went over to the cabin. Leif gave him some soup and watched him eat from across the table.

"How come you watching me?" Soapy grumbled.

"It's my damn house and I'll watch whatever I please. I think its time you start explaining yourself anyway. Why were you stealing my horse?"

"I didn't steal your horse. I was just – stuck out here, looking for somewhere warm."

Leif just looked at him. If the little weasel didn't start talking straight, he was gonna throw him over his shoulder and bring him back out to the pit for another night.

"All right, all right, I was gonna steal your horses."

"Horse-s. You was gonna steal all of an old man's horses. What kind of person are you then?"

Soapy didn't take this well. He dropped his spoon and started sputtering. "I don't...you can't know what it's like. I'm not bein' mean, jus'...I gotta get out of there. I got nuthin' for me here... Nuthin."

Leif looked less than sympathetic.

"You met my momma? Huh, mister?" Soapy leaned in. "You think I can get any respect in that town? You think I could ever get a *woman* in that town?" He was getting progressively louder and shriller. "You got no idea what it's like, you'd steal a million horses to get outta my situation!" He was practically shouting now.

"Who's goin' out with you?" he asked.

"No one." Soapy looked down.

"Is it Tali?"

"Pfft. I wish."

Leif raised his eyebrows.

"Ain't Tali. S'at other one. The woman that stays with her."

"Oh, the Outsider. Libby, right?"

"Yeah, I guess." Soapy looked deflated. He usually looked so puffy and proud.

Leif thought how that woman was probably being treated in town. She was probably a pariah. He knew how that went. He knew how those people could be. So bad that she'd agree to cross the glacier with this weasel in the middle of winter. He figured she must be mighty miserable.

"Tell you what. I'm gonna take you back to town so your momma can fix up your leg, but let me tell you something." Leif paused for dramatic effect. This speech needed to have impact. He could not deal with the threat of thieving in addition to all the other perils of life on his own in this part of the world. "You've used up all the mercy I've got. I see you out here again death'll be the best thing you can hope for outta me. You got that?"

Soapy looked down. That was not enough to placate Leif.

"Do. You. Understand?"

"Yeah, I know, all right, I won't come back."

Soapy ate and warmed up, Leif took him back out to the barn and loaded him up on Shadow. The two men didn't talk as they walked toward town, Soapy on Shadow and Leif alongside. Soapy managed not to complain about his leg the entire time.

The men arrived at the village well past dark, greeted by quiet streets and glowing houses. Leif took Soapy home. When he got outside the house, Leif went up toward the door. Soapy started hollering to let him off the horse but Leif ignored him. He banged on the door and Chena opened up.

"What?"

"Brought back your boy." He nodded toward the horse.

"Did ya now." She glared at Soapy.

"I ain't bringin' him back next time he comes out my way, if you know what I mean."

She looked at him coldly. "I reckon I do."

"Well, then come get him off the horse."

Her and Leif helped Soapy off the horse. As Leif hopped on Shadow and started off, he could hear Chena start in on her son. Leif chuckled to himself. A boy would gnaw off his arm off to get away from mothering like that.

Leif stopped by Tali's on the way out of town. She offered him to stay with it being so late but he declined. He had his chickens and Shadow's foal to get back to. He did tell her that if Libby wanted to come and stay with him until spring that it'd be all right, not that his cabin had much to offer. Tali agreed to relay the message. She tried to push some food off on him but he managed to rush off unencumbered.

Leif enjoyed his ride home, watching the stars until the moon came up, and then the moon until he got home.

45

Tali had been enjoying having Libby stay with her. It was nice to have someone to talk to. It was nice having a friend.

On this particular morning, Tali went over to the main house for work early in the morning. She unbundled in the kitchen and started work on the fire. After finishing with the stove, she went out to the root cellar to fetch a load of food.

She crossed the yard and went in the root cellar. The doors were not barred, and she suspected there was someone inside. Indeed, upon opening the second door, Tali found Qaniit curled up on a crate, wrapped in a blanket with her knees to her chest, looking positively miserable.

Tali immediately worried that Qaniit had found out about her and Kilaun. Panic-stricken, she asked, "Qaniit, what's wrong?"

Qaniit looked at her, eyes bloodshot and tired. She was in a fragile state and about to break. Tali stood like wood, tall and frozen, waiting for the inevitable.

"I'm pregnant." A wave of relief hit Tali, who quite immediately felt guilty for feeling relieved when Qaniit was feeling so unhappy. Tali sat kneeled down in front of her.

"I thought you might want another child," Tali said.

"Kilaun sure does," Qaniit sniffled.

"You don't?"

"I don't want anything anymore." Qaniit breathed in deep and looked up. "Other than something else."

After a pause, Tali responded, "There isn't anything else, is there?" She hadn't been feeling particularly happy herself for a long while. Things had been better since Kilaun had lost interest in her, and Libby came to stay with her, but still not all that good. Just better.

"There's nothing," Qaniit said flatly. "Just eating and hauling water and sitting on this crate. I wait for every day to pass just like the one before."

"Oh, Qaniit..." Tali shifted to sit and leaned her head on Qaniit's legs.

The women didn't say anything for a minute. Qaniit breathed heavy.

"What are you going to do?" Tali asked her.

"I don't know. I don't—"

Tali looked at her and cocked her head.

"I don't want Chu to know."

Tali had seen how much affection Qaniit had for Chu, but she hadn't put together there was a relationship between them. "It is Kilaun's?"

"Of course. I have never been unfaithful. But, still – I just –"

"You can't help who you love, Qaniit."

"I don't love Kilaun. I don't want him. I don't want his child."

Tali wished she could tell her how well she understood, but she couldn't. She just said, "I understand," and looked down.

After a silence, Qaniit said quietly, "I knew about you two."

Tali looked up at her, trying to maintain a blank expression.

"I knew."

"Why—Qaniit, … I'm sorry."

"No, I'm sorry. I should have protected you better."

"Protected me? It's my fault, I should have – done something different."

"We live every day, doing things, and they could all be done different. This isn't the world I wanted for myself, and it's not the world I want for a child."

"Chena could help you."

Qaniit furrowed her brow, asking how so.

"She helped me once," Tali lowered her eyes.

Qaniit leg go of her legs and reached out to hug Tali. Tali hugged her back, and started crying. She felt terrible for lying to Qaniit, for being unfaithful to her, for just everything.

"Oh, don't cry. We're all wretched now. Every last one of us."

Tali pulled back, wiping her face with her sleeve.

"Let's stop being wretched, Qaniit. Let's figure something better."

Qaniit studied her.

"There's no harm in trying, I suppose," she smiled weakly.

The women gathered the potatoes and the vegetables and headed back in the house, the faint traces of tears freezing on their cheeks in the short walk across the yard.

46

Kilaun knew that the hour was what he might have previously considered bedtime. He'd once had a habit of washing his face before going to sleep, but he'd recently abandoned the practice. He also no longer wore clothing in bed. It was part punishment, part concession. A punishment for the wild, uncontrolled thoughts that had been creeping up and springing upon his mind. A concession to the part of him that had always known he was a wild creature and had no place in civilization.

The Kilaun of this day understood little of the humans around him. Were all people like this? Fickle? Duplicitous? He felt more of an affinity for the creatures of the wild: the bear, the moose, and the wolf. Especially the wolf. Surely, wolves did not abandon their families. You always knew where you stood with wild creatures.

His wife was nowhere to be seen. His brother was nowhere to be seen. The cook, the maid, and the world – they had all left him. He felt utterly alone.

And so, as Kilaun pictured it, he was ethical, industrious and noble like the wolf, but he had been betrayed, abandoned, double-crossed by a faithless pack. He had assumed the others to be wolf-like, as he was. But they were humans all the way through, that vile species that constructed the governments of murder and pillage and rape that Kilaun so despised.

These people didn't even deserve the town Kilaun had built them.

The house grew cold because he did not feed the fire. He grew hungry but did not eat. This was not punishment for him, it was punishment for them. They'd be sorry if they knew how he suffered. They would find out and maybe they would change their ways.

Kilaun walked the dark house cold, hungry, and naked. It was his house, his planet, and he would walk it however he wanted to. The people all around him had become humans. They were no better than those humans on the mainland.

He fetched tobacco from his office and rolled a cigarette. It was his last paper. He was sure to be displeased in the morning. But, in the same way he had no respect for the others, he had no respect for himself, and besides, what had all his discipline gotten him? So he'd have one more thing to suffer tomorrow. Fine.

Kilaun went and stood by the window while he smoked his cigarette. The townsfolk were asleep. They slept in their soft little beds, with tummies full of food they had not hunted or gathered, in their little village, apart from nature, as though they were above it. The village he used to feel so loyal to. Just a bunch of humans. Weak, selfish, and soft. Nature would not have allowed them to survive. It was only due to Kilaun's efforts that these creatures remained here, here and alive, and he felt sorry for it. Better, perhaps, to have let nature take its course.

He walked to the guest room. No Chu. Where was the brother? Not here. He stared at the bed. It was the bed that he had dreamt about. He realized that Chu might well be out planning his murder. Probably his wife was with him, perhaps they were lying together naked, discussing how best to end Kilaun's life. And who knew which others of the townspeople were part of the plot as well. He had done so much for them all. He saw now that he'd never had a chance. It was simply their nature. The nature of humans.

The snow piled higher as he smoked. He dropped the cigarette when it became so small that it burned his finger and simply walked off as though he were outside, unconcerned about where it landed.

He went and lay down in his bedroom. Not in the bed, but on the floor. He pushed back the braided rug, that damned rug, and felt the cold, hand-hewn planks against his back. He had made those planks with his own hands. Everything he'd done right in this life he'd done with his own hands. His cursed, human hands.

Kilaun felt cold inside, like the animal he believed he was. He fell fast asleep in his loneliness, facing up to the ceiling, ready to do battle from his back if necessary.

The cold, dead eyes of a predator awaited him in his dreamspace. They watched him enter his dreams. He saw them watching him, waiting for him, blinking, the way cold, dead eyes always do. As he descended into the dreamworld, he saw that the eyes were his own. They widened, and his lips parted to speak, but only a whisper escaped. A whisper he could not understand.

He was in a hallway walled by giant stone blocks, each carefully fitted together. He could feel their age, knew they were ancient, a thousand years, or a million, or maybe they had been born with the earth.

Kilaun's dreaming self sensed that time was not how he perceived it in his waking hours. It presented the illusion of perfect linearity, but the reality was that it was more of a looping, circling thing, building thing, like yarn wrapping into a ball, constantly covering over the other yarn and crisscrossing itself endlessly. If the yarn was continually wrapped in the same direction over and over, the ball would become lopsided and untenable. You had to change course.

Kilaun had not changed course in a long time. Instead, the course he had chosen had changed him.

He realized that he was no longer in that hallway, but instead in a different one that looked exactly the same. But now it was day, not night, although there were no windows to see the outside. Fear struck him suddenly and he ran, ran hard, untiring, down the hall. He ran and ran, and it turned and he ran, but it was the same hallway, just some other place.

The dream changed again. He was watching a dog happily chewing on something. The ears…it was a rabbit. The severed head of a rabbit. The dog chewed enthusiastically, his lips pulled back in what looked very much like a wry smile. A human-like rabbit eyeball had come loose, fallen from its socket, but connective tissue forced it to hang there, watchful, swaying, as the dog's powerful jaws worked at the head the eyeball had just before been a part of. The eyeball swung with a familiar rhythm – it was something he had seen before.

Kilaun was steering a boat now. He hadn't steered a boat in many years. There was a child crying, a baby in the background, but that was not his business, he had to attend to the steering. The weather was foul and looked to be getting worse. The rain grew heavier, thunder grew louder, and waves grew taller. And the baby cried and wailed on in the distance. Was he alone on the boat? Or was the human child there with him?

The child was drowning. Water rushing in the bow of the boat, filling the floor and the cabinets and onto the bed with the baby. It cried as the water filled up around it. It floated at first, and flipped onto its belly. It was the smallest infant, and it did not flip itself back over. The human child was face down in the water. Crying into the water, water creeping into its little fragile body and filling its lungs. It cried until it died and then was dead. The lifeless, limp, human child floated in the water facedown. It floated from the cabin into the hallway, bounced against the door of the head and floated into the kitchen, flooded counter-high. The tiny corpse lodged in between a monkey-shaped banana hanger screwed into the counter and the mini-fridge that hadn't kept anything cold in many years. And still, Kilaun steered the boat.

Kilaun floated in and out of his dreams, and he saw these were the dreams the ancestors gave him. He knew they spoke to him. He knew that his wife was pregnant and that, if he did not stop her, she would drown his infant child.

47

Soapy found Libby at the spring again. She was filling buckets with water. It had been thirty below for weeks, and getting water first involved smashing through the ice with a metal rod that was left nearby.

Soapy approached her, trying to walk as normally as possible. Now, added to his half-mutilated toe, he had an injured leg. His mother informed him a number of times that he was lucky it wasn't broken, that it wasn't *that* bad, and that it really couldn't hurt that badly, but she didn't know about his plans. It *was* that bad if it affected his plans to leave the village and go south.

He was ready though, and he wasn't going to let his gimpy leg stop him. The Outsider was his only potential connection to the mainland, and he needed to take advantage of the opportunity to take her home. As much as he would be her guide over the glacier, she would be his past the Port.

"Libby," he whispered. She jumped.

"Jesus, Soapy." She pursed her lips. "Why are you whispering?" She sounded annoyed, and turned back to her buckets.

"I wasn't." Yes, he was, but he wasn't sure why. Because he was trying to sneak up on her, probably, and then forgot he wasn't sneaking anymore. He was sure there was a reason, he just couldn't think of it.

"Are you ready to get out of here?" he asked her, smiling wide, showing his missing teeth.

She sighed and shook her head as she pulled the bucket out of the water. "You've got to be kidding."

He furrowed his brow inquisitively.

"You think I didn't hear you tried to steal Leif's horses and broke your leg in the process? Bet you're barely standing right now." Her voice had taken on the tone of condescension that Soapy was all too used to from the rest of the townsfolk.

"Right, I'm walking around on a bum leg, sure. I figured being from Outside you wouldn't be taken in by all the stupidity you hear from folks around here, but I guess I was wrong. My leg's good enough to do what I have to."

She snapped the lids on her buckets. "What you have to? Seems like whether it was your leg or your head, something wasn't good enough to get those horses." She spoke quickly, allowing him no opportunity to interject. "And stealing horses from an old man who needs them doesn't exactly make me trust you, not to mention the fact that you couldn't even manage to get them. Also, it's obvious those horses were your plan for getting across the glacier, and not only do you not have horses now, you can barely walk. Is your new plan for me to carry you?"

She picked up the buckets and started marching across the yard as quickly as she could, anxious to escape the cold, the conversation, and the feeling that her shoulders would tear loose from their sockets from the weight of the water.

"Plus, in case you didn't notice, it's colder than hell out here. I can think of better ways to die than freezing to death on a glacier with you."

Soapy jumped in front of her. He was starting to panic. He had spent too much time thinking and planning for this to not work.

"But you made a deal!"

"I *what*?" She let the buckets drop to the ground.

"To hire me to guide you across the glacier."

"You've got to be kidding."

"Look, you made a deal. You need to keep that deal." He started to get angry and stood closer to her.

"Or what, Soapy?" She backed up a bit. He got closer.

"Or there will be consequences."

Libby's feet backed into a low stump. "Look, you're standing a little close to me right now and it's making me feel threatened."

Soapy's pulse started to race, and adrenaline hit him. "Oh, you're feeling threatened?" He leaned in toward her. "Well, maybe you need to back up then."

She glanced back at the stump and managed to stumble around it.

"What do you want?" she asked.

"You have until Friday," Soapy said.

"To what?" she asked, incredulous.

"To get your stuff together to go."

"It's not going to happen," she said, contemptuously.

"There are consequences to every action."

She just looked at him, without expression.

"So you have until Friday, or there will be consequences."

Libby reached down for her buckets and Soapy saw her hands were shaking. It only made him more indignant.

"Friday," he said. And with that, he stormed off.

48

Chena found Kilaun naked on the floor again. The rug was pushed up against the wall like a discarded towel. He was dead to the world. His upper half was flat on his back, arms flailed about to either side, while his lower half turned sideways, his genitals flopping about miserably.

But it was nothing she hadn't seen before.

She pushed back the curtains but there was little light to come in. The winter had faded into days of darkness, interrupted by a few hours of twilight. Other people hated this time of year, but Chena never minded it. Wishing things were some other way than the way they were was a fool's pursuit in her mind.

Kilaun stirred a bit and mumbled. Chena grabbed a blanket off the bed and threw it over his clumsy, naked body. The bed was still warm. Qaniit must have slept in it the night before, and wasn't long gone. It was frigid cold in the room though. Chena was starting to think the household was going to hell. How could a man sleep naked on the freezing cold floor, and how could his supposed wife step right over him to climb in the bed and not even throw a damned blanket over him?

"There's only so much I can do, you know," she bitched. "I'm here most of the day. I feed you, I keep the fire going, I haul the water, and I take care of everything like a mother. All you have to do, the tiny little thing that you have to do, is to keep the fire going when I'm not here. If you can keep your clothes on, all the better, but I'm not even asking that." She squatted down next to Kilaun as much as she could squat at her age. "You hear me?" She poked him through the blanket.

He mumbled something incomprehensible, eyes still closed, and she stood back up. "Get up," she said, and left the room, leaving the door open behind her.

*

Chena was frying some blue potatoes when Kilaun meandered into the kitchen.

"Nice of you to join us here in the civilized world," she snapped. "Oh, and pants!" She looked down at Kilaun's lower half. "You really do care."

Kilaun grumbled something about humans, then, "Where's my wife?"

"How am I supposed to know?" Chena snorted. "If I can't keep you in check, I certainly can't keep track of her. You people are adults, so why don't you ever talk to one another. She probably run off with your damn brother is where she probably is."

Kilaun roared and pushed Chena against the wall. She was quickly and thoroughly terrified. Goodness gracious, he'd gone out of his mind indeed. "What do you know?" he roared.

"Nothing!" she stuttered, "I don't know – it's just – maybe they shouldn't spend so much time together!"

He let her go and returned to his grumbling introspection. Chena stood breathing heavy while he picked at fried potatoes from the pan as if he had not just acted a fool. Chena had seen him go after Tali with his anger, but never her. He hadn't been right at all.

"She's pregnant?" he asked.

Chena's eyes widened. She didn't know, but didn't know whether to say she didn't know. He might think she was lying. She didn't want to get him all worked up. She had her point of view and knew what it was but she was still an old woman who couldn't afford a broken hip over someone else's drama and nonsense. So she kept her mouth shut.

"I know it anyway. You don't have to tell me." He started out the back door then hesitated, "Oh, when you see my wife, tell her we need to talk." Kilaun smiled in a calm and indifferent way that chilled Chena's bones. She went back to the potatoes, and pushed past wondering whether he had lost his mind entirely.

49

Chu had not slept at Kilaun's the night before. He slept at Tali's cabin on the cot in the living room. Tali slept in the back room with Libby. Kilaun had been behaving strangely, and it worried Chu. Worried him enough that he felt as though it was better to stay at Tali's.

Lately, when in his brother's company, Chu would catch Kilaun staring at him, his face a mask of loathing and rage. Sometimes Kilaun would quickly look away. But at other times, looking over had no effect. It was as though Kilaun didn't recognize Chu or he thought he was invisible and he would just continue to stare directly at Chu. And there was the talking to himself. Kilaun muttered and mumbled under his breath constantly. Chu wasn't even sure his brother was making any words, just noises, but whatever the case the tone conveyed only hostility and hatred.

Tali had said Chu could stay at her place whenever he wanted. He figured he would take her up on it until Kilaun returned to normal.

He spent the morning helping out at Tali's. Chu could do an incredible amount of work in a very short time, and his efforts chopping wood and carrying water saved his hosts a lot of effort. Tali fixed some food to reward his efforts. Chu would have needed four or five helpings to get full, but he limited himself to only one, as he could see the stores were thin. Qaniit stopped by as they were eating. She did not seem upset that Chu had stayed there. Nobody spoke about why he did so, but he knew that Qaniit had seen what he'd seen in Kilaun too.

Chu left with Qaniit to walk back over to the house.

"You don't have to be afraid of him, you know," she told him.

Chu remained silent.

They took the long way home, walking on the back road. Soapy was out clearing snow off Chena's roof. He grumbled as he stood on top of a wobbly steel barrel. Chu went and held it steady for him. Qaniit waited and watched. She wasn't particularly eager to get home, despite the cold.

When he was done, they kept on walking in silence. The town was quiet. It had to be, with this kind of cold. Everyone stayed inside as much as they could, leaving only to perform the most vital tasks. There wasn't much beyond wood, water and food that made it worth leaving the house.

Eventually Chu broke the silence. "I'm not," he said. Qaniit, now used to Chu's habits, took only a moment to recall what they last talked about. "I don't think he knows who I am sometimes."

A few moments later he added, "He's my brother."

With Chu there was usually a lot left unsaid, but Qaniit filled in the blanks. If Chu had to defend himself, at least one of the two brothers would get hurt, and no matter what happened, Chu loved his brother and wanted to protect him. Qaniit wondered if Chu would even strike his brother to defend himself. She wasn't sure.

Then they were silent again. Even with her face obscured by a thick scarf she looked pretty, her little brown eyes peeking through her wrappings. Like a present. Chu started thinking back to Christmas.

"We should have Christmas, Qaniit," he said.

She smiled. "We should." She stepped closer to him and put her arm through his, and they walked in the snow. Chu liked having her close to him.

They rounded the corner over by the spring and nearly ran square into Kilaun. Qaniit jumped, exclaiming, "Jesus, where are you going so fast?"

"To find you, Wife." He turned to Chu, "And you, Brother." He spoke oddly, mechanically, with alert eyes fixed forward, moved by vulture-like tilting of his head.

Chu looked at Qaniit, who didn't look concerned. She didn't look anything. She wore a blank face, looking vacantly ahead. She dumbly withdrew her arm from his. Chu worried for her.

"What is it?" Chu asked, turning to Kilaun.

"It's time for you to go," he responded.

Qaniit interrupted, "Kilaun, what are you doing?"

"I am doing the right thing. I will no longer have your poisonous human presence trying to take my village, trying to take my wife." Kilaun wore a lesser version of the hateful expression. There was still some of his intellect in it.

Chu had started to tell his brother that he didn't understand, but Qaniit loudly trampled his gentle attempt at words. "Kilaun, you don't own this village and you don't own me."

Kilaun smiled thinly and tilted his head slightly to the side, staring intently at his wife. "I own you as long as you carry my child inside you," he said, icily.

Chu looked at Qaniit, and she looked down.

"Oh, *Brother*, you didn't know?" Kilaun asked, spitefully.

Chu began to speak, "Kilaun, I know you have not felt well lately, but—", but he was cut off by Kilaun.

"There is nothing wrong with me. This is the first day I am feeling right. The ancestors have given me a vision. They have told me about both of you. You, Brother, they have said are trying to drain me of my life. You are trying to take away my village and my wife, and you may have neither. You, Wife, they have told me that you will kill my child if I do not stop you. And I will stop you both, one way or another."

Chu stepped toward his brother, wearing a look of sadness. "Kilaun, you are wrong. That does not make sense."

"You will leave this town."

"To where?"

"Somewhere else. You will leave this town."

Qaniit stepped forward, "Kilaun, you're being crazy. No one can get out right now, and Chu isn't doing anything against you. He's not trying to steal anything from you." Kilaun was glowering at Chu. If his wife's words registered, he showed no sign of it. "He's your brother. You can't do that to your brother!"

His hard stare remained focused on Chu. And then, abruptly, he turned around and briskly returned in the direction from which he'd come.

Qaniit, left alone with Chu, stared at her feet and shivered. She could not break the silence. She did not know what to say, or where to start.

But it was Chu who spoke. "He's gone. That is not my brother." He watched Kilaun walk off into the distance. "He is someone else now."

Qaniit realized then what she needed to know. "You won't leave, will you?" She turned to face him. To be left with Kilaun, without Chu, it was not a life she could bear.

"No. I cannot leave now. My brother is gone and that…that person is here instead. You need protection from that person..." After a few moments he added, "You are with child. Why did you not say so?"

She fumbled with her scarf. "I was ashamed."

"He is your husband."

"But he is not who I love."

Chu said nothing. She loved him? Did she mean that? The idea was simultaneously the most wonderful and most horrible thing he could imagine.

"Do you want to leave this place?" he asked.

"I've wanted to leave for a long time."

"Then we will. In two days."

"Chu… No one can leave here. It's the middle of winter."

"Do you trust me?"

"I do."

"I walked thousands of miles to this place. I would not say we could leave here if I were not sure."

She pressed her lips together and almost imperceptibly nodded her head.

50

Libby felt shaken after her confrontation with Soapy at the spring, but was too embarrassed of agreeing to leave with him to tell Tali or anyone else about it.

If Libby wanted to leave before, she really wanted to leave now. So when Tali told her that Leif offered for Libby to go stay with him, Libby felt like a huge weight had been lifted from her shoulders. Tali had been good to her and was a pleasant enough person to live with, but the feeling of being an outsider had cemented itself rather than softened over time. Tali, Chu, and Qaniit were the only people in town that treated her like a human being. The rest avoided meeting her gaze, but when her eyes looked elsewhere she could feel their suspicious stares following her around.

Libby, in her surprise, said something about packing before she realized that she owned nothing of her own to take with her. Tali gave her a couple of pieces of clothing. Libby could tell the younger woman was trying her hardest to suppress sadness at the thought of Libby's departure. The pair made a bit of a ceremony out of packing up the clothes and a few personal items that Libby had collected. The boots would have to be returned in a few months, but by then Libby could figure something else out. Tali told her that Leif could make her some mukluks if he had hide to spare. It hardly mattered. Leif wouldn't let her suffer any more than she had to.

Moving into a house alone with a stranger in the woods was not an entirely pleasant thought, but even if she were miserable out there at least it'd be a novel form of misery. But Tali's assurances went a long way toward making Libby feel comfortable with the idea, and Tali mentioned that Libby could come right back if she wanted several more times than was necessary. Libby felt sorry for the girl.

Libby didn't tell anyone other than Tali that she was leaving and asked Tali not to tell anyone either. Libby didn't want Soapy coming and confronting her, or worse yet, trailing her. She just wanted to slip off into the woods like nothing ever happened.

The possibility of Kilaun stopping her if he heard had also occurred to her and struck her as an even less pleasant possibility than another confrontation with Soapy. She had some awareness of Leif's history with Kilaun and, while not getting along with Kilaun seemed like good sign regarding his character, if Kilaun caught wind of her going there, he might not like it.

Tali and her left early in the morning, traveling by foot up the old logging road. Gun came with them, dragging a sled with some food and supplies. Without knowing how much Leif had put away for the winter, Tali insisted on Libby bringing some things to help out. It was clear she and the older man cared for one another very much.

For a while, they chatted, but it was a long walk and it was cold and there was a heaviness to the mood they shared. Libby thought back to her time in the basement prison, freezing and starving. That place was just a few hundred feet from Tali's. She felt its presence in every moment she spent in the village. Now that feeling was fading.

The fear of the townspeople remained. The fear engendered by their fear of her. Would they be relieved to find her gone? Or would they see it as a threat, a precursor to her bringing forth some kind of government army to have them all destroyed?

They'd been traveling for nearly two hours when it began to snow. It made Libby feel even further from the village. Safer. But Gun was already tired, and fresh snow made the going more difficult than the hard packed mass that had been solidly underfoot up until then.

"Why would he want to live so far away? Before all this stuff with the horses, at least?"

"He'd live farther if he weren't already backed up against the glacier," Tali said, breathing heavily from the hike.

"Does he not like being around people or something? Is he going to be annoyed having me around?"

"Oh, no, no. He's fine with people, or at least he used to be. He mainly doesn't like Kilaun."

At the mention of Kilaun, they both fell silent, each lapsing into ruminations of the suffering he'd caused them. They walked quietly in the trees and falling snow, taking care to not outpace poor Gun.

Eventually, Libby's curiosity regarding her new roommate forced her to talk again.

"Why doesn't he at least come into town? To trade, or whatever?"

"He used to." Tali paused to catch her breath before continuing. When she resumed speaking, it was more quietly. "Leif blamed Kilaun for my father's death. They didn't get along either. My father and Kilaun, I mean. Leif...I guess he sort of picked up the torch when my father died."

"Was is his fault? Kilaun's, I mean."

Tali was silent for several moments, and Libby wondered if she was wrong to ask.

"No, I don't think so."

They trudged on for another minute before Tali added, "It was his heart, they said. Father was very intense...very serious. But he didn't hate Kilaun. They just disagreed.

"Kilaun wasn't always like this, I guess. I mean, he was serious but it was about how people should live. He just wanted the town to work and to be great."

She looked away and sighed deeply.

"But now...now he's so paranoid. Afraid of everything but what he can control. It's like he cares about the village but not the people."

Libby responded, "I feel sorry for Qaniit, stuck with him like that. She seems like the type that'd leave rather than put up with him."

"Yeah," was all Tali could muster.

Libby was fairly certain that Kilaun and Tali had been fooling around and hadn't meant to poke at a sore spot. A good-looking and powerful man, she could see the appeal, especially to a young woman whose sole relative had died. And Libby hadn't lived the life of a saint herself.

"Libby?" Tali sounded tentative. "Are you going to go...you know...back? Outside?

Libby pondered how best to answer for a moment. "I don't know. I hope so, I think. I know it sounds silly, but I felt like things might have been starting to get better. People were starting to feel sort of hopeful again. I'm curious to see what things are like now. If things are improving...I don't know. I guess I'd want to be a part of that."

Gun passed them. Apparently, he'd come to the realization that they were close to Leif's and it gave him a burst of energy. He turned onto the path and the women followed.

Libby continued, "But I really don't know. It could've all gone to hell the instant I left, I have no idea. If I don't go back, well, I doubt I can stay with Leif forever, and I know your village doesn't like me much."

"We're nearly there," Tali said.

"What about you? Would you want to go?"

"Outside? Me?" Tali thought about it for what appeared to Libby to be for the first time. "Even if I wanted to, I'm just here.

I'm here." She waved her hand to her surroundings. Libby saw that even if Tali hated it, this was her home.

They approached the stable first and then the cabin. Libby was pleased by the looks of the place. There was smoke coming from the cabin's chimney, and a view of the mountains and moraine. The place looked well cared-for, and she could hear chickens making noise in the back behind the house. It was more homey than anywhere she'd been in a long time.

Tali called out to Leif, who came out. He took the sled off the worn out dog who still had enough energy to bolt directly to the door, making his wishes known. Leif invited everyone in. Libby felt welcome, though nervous about Tali's departure.

Tali stayed with them for a few hours. Leif fed them all stew and Libby thought it might have been the most delicious thing she'd had since she'd set out from home. Or what had been home.

Leif told Libby that the loft was hers and that he'd stay downstairs on the palette but she insisted upon reversing the situation, refusing the more comfortable accommodations on the pretense that she was afraid of falling from the loft. She was grateful and she wanted to make sure that she was welcome here for as long as possible.

Nobody made a fuss when Tali left, acting as though she were just walking a few feet home and they'd all see each other tomorrow, but Libby knew that Tali was sad to leave her companion, and Tali knew that Libby was nervous to live with a man she did not know. The sound of their goodbyes was the last sound in the cabin for a long while. Libby and Leif sat by the fire. At first the silence felt awkward but, at some point, without noticing, each retreated into their private thoughts and the awkwardness was forgotten.

51

The day after the confrontation with Chu, Kilaun laid very low. He stayed in bed all morning, and not even Chena could rouse him. Qaniit tiptoed around on alert for signs of life from her husband, while Chu secretly got things together for their trip. She did not look at him when they passed one another, in fear that their scheme would rip through the veil of secrecy and they would suddenly be exposed as deserters.

She was fixing tea in the kitchen when he passed through. She tried to look occupied.

"Chu, stop going in and out the house," Chena barked, managing to sound somewhat less peevish than usual. "It's cold out there and if I get sick, I'll probably keel over dead. Do you want that on your conscience?"

Chu smiled, "If you help me clean up the shed then I'll only have to go in and out half as much."

"Get!" she hollered, possibly with a tone of mild amusement.

Qaniit heard Kilaun stirring in the back of the house.

"Guess the king has risen," Chena muttered.

Within a minute, the front door slammed. Qaniit went to the window and saw Kilaun headed north out of town. She surmised he was headed to the ridge. Chu was still out in the shed as far as she knew.

Qaniit waited until her husband had been gone for several minutes, departing the kitchen with as much nonchalance as she could muster, then quickly and silently making her way to the office. Knives, tobacco, trinkets...anything of value might be the difference between life and death outside the village. She wouldn't take it yet, but it would be good to know what was there and where it was in case she had less time when the time really came to grab and go.

She'd made her way to the office quite stealthily, listening carefully to be sure Chena hadn't come near and Kilaun hadn't returned. When she attempted to turn the knob, it didn't budge. Locked.

With her annoyance came the abandonment of silence and secrecy. She yelled for Chena and then muttered to herself as she made her way back toward the kitchen. "Chena! Why is the office door locked?" She stood staring at the older woman, hands on her hips.

Chena looked at her contemptuously. "You think I know? I just work here. I don't pretend to be able to keep all you crazy people in line. Why Kilaun locks the door on his office is his business."

Qaniit looked at her blankly and said, "I want it open."

"Well then open it! Ain't got nothing to do with me."

"Chena, who do you think is going to hear the most about it if I break the door trying to get in?"

Chena sighed and wiped off her hands. "Fine." She opened the cupboard that used to store Qaniit's secret stash of jelly and reached far in the back, pulling out a key. She thrust it at Qaniit. "You stole it as far as I'm concerned."

"Thank you, Chena," Qaniit curtseyed like a child and off she went.

Looking out the window to make sure her husband was nowhere in sight, she unlocked the door to his office. As she started opening it, an odor hit her. Revolted, she held her nose and proceeded in the room. It reeked.

Qaniit looked around and saw a few piles of wrapped packages at the backside of the room – on the chair, on the floor, and on a table. Still holding her nose, she pulled back the fabric on the package on the chair and recoiled. Behind the fabric was dark, rotten flesh. She kicked the sack on the floor and knew it held the same thing.

She ran back to the kitchen, still holding her nose, and exclaimed, "Chena! What the hell is going on?"

Chena looked legitimately baffled and followed Qaniit back to the office. Chena attempted an air of detached condescension as she unwrapped the meat on the chair. Qaniit stood at the back of the room. Without even fully unwrapping the meat it was clear that it was teeming with maggots.

"My God, he's really lost it," the old woman said, more to herself than to Qaniit. The two of them stood quietly, not knowing what to do.

"What is it?" Qaniit asked.

"Wolf, I'd guess." Chena plucked a tuft of gray and white fur from the floor, dried blood and skin still stuck to the other end of it.

Chena stood there thinking, Qaniit still horrified, with her shirt pulled over her nose. Qaniit blurted out, "Let's get Chu."

Chena held her hand up as if to tell Qaniit to wait. She finally said, "I don't think he ought be here when Kilaun gets back." Already concerned, Qaniit grew even more alarmed to see Chena's expression.

"He asked me for his gun. Last night, he wanted the Colt. He said he was going to shoot a rat. I thought, I don't know, I didn't think much of it, he's a crazy man. But this morning when I tried to wake him, he was mumbling, he said something about Chu, and I started to wonder. He's got a gun and he's gone mad, and if anyone's going to get it...." Chena pointed to the desk and Qaniit saw .45 bullets scattered about carelessly.

It suddenly made sense to Qaniit. Kilaun had been getting increasingly jealous, finally asking Chu to leave altogether. And here Chu goes refusing to leave. They didn't have much ammo, and Kilaun wouldn't use it unless... Damn Chena for giving him the gun!

Without a word, Qaniit took off at full speed toward the shed. She tore the thin aluminum door open but found the shed empty. She sped back to the house, looking everywhere at once for a sign, a clue, of where Chu could be. Chena walked slowly into the hallway and watched Qaniit blankly, still holding that blood encrusted tuft of fur.

Qaniit ran back outside and saw Soapy dragging a log across the town, stumbling along despite his bad leg. "Soapy!" He kept dragging.

"Have you seen Chu?" she asked, breathless. He grunted, and barely looked up at her. She screamed at him, "Chu! Have you seen him?"

Soapy snorted, "He was headed up to the ridge. Probably off to check his traps."

Qaniit gasped. That meant her husband and Chu were both on that ridge and only Kilaun was armed.

"You know, you ought have a talk with him about how he lays his traps. He's liable to get himself in trouble someday runnin' em parallel to other men's!"

Qaniit was scarcely aware he was still speaking. She was already running back to the house to get her coat. She had to get to the ridge.

52

Chu finished his work at the house and went to check his traps.

The trap line ran straight up the ridge side. It would have been all but impassable to most, but Chu's long strides made no concessions to the terrain and he scaled the hillside rapidly, tracing a route he recognized solely by the contours of the snow.

The first few traps were empty. Chu picked them up and carried them with him. He would not want an animal to get caught and killed for no purpose. He planned to leave the following day, with Qaniit, so he would take care of these things before he left. Any meat he pulled out of his traps today would go on the trip with them.

The fourth had a rabbit. He field dressed it and roped it to his belt. The next few, nothing. Then a lynx. That was a good catch. He continued up the hillside, taking up the traps. By the top he had enough meat to get them across the glacier, and he was carrying a heavy load of traps.

Chu had run his traps parallel to Soapy's, true enough. Now he wanted to bring his traps over to Soapy's last trap, and leave them there, disarmed. Then, when Soapy checked his traps the next day, at the end of the morning, he would find the traps. No sense in good traps going to waste, and it perhaps it would take the edge off the bitterness the little man always seemed to be feeling.

Chu started cutting across the hillside, high up on the ridge, through deep snow, and weighted down with his traps and his catch. It was difficult going, even for Chu. It started to flurry. It was slow going, and he knew cutting across would take at least an hour at this rate but, having settled on a course of action, physical discomfort or difficulty was rarely enough to change his mind.

Chu felt bad for leaving the townspeople. No one grows up thinking about what it would be like to be poor, starving, having no contact with the rest of the world. These people, most of them, were from somewhere else, where they had a better life, somewhere that didn't exist anymore. Chu understood this was hard, which is why he did not blame them for mistakes like what they did to Libby.

But he could not stay and Qaniit could not stay. She had been good to him and good *for* him and he felt life would be different from now on. She respected him, she valued him for more than his capacity for work. Seeing himself the way she saw him changed his perception. Chu was aware that he loved her, but he was not bothered by the uncertainty and ambiguity of their situation. It was enough that he would travel with her, that he could protect her. To be of use to her was enough, if the reward was to be in her company.

He would have been content to be second in her life, but Kilaun's increasing paranoia had ruined it. The ancestors spoke to Kilaun, but he did not seem to pay any heed to those who were still living. Perhaps speaking to the ancestors was what had destroyed him, perhaps he had become enslaved by their message.

They had never spoken to Chu, and he had often deferred to Kilaun because surely they had chosen Kilaun for a reason. But if Kilaun was behaving according to the wishes of the ancestors now, then Chu was glad they had not chosen him. You did not have to be a smart man to know what was right. You should not need ancestors or gods or priests or other men to tell you.

Chu trudged through the snow, and despite all the turmoil in his life, was more focused on marveling at the world around him than on any potential sources of anxiety. There weren't too many trees at this height, just some alders and the occasional renegade spruce or aspen. When the aspens grew at this elevation, they grew small and twisted and furious. The black spruce looked like trees he had seen in a book with drawings once. Tall, thin trunks with sporadic burls, appearing for small, extravagant performances. The environment was harsh, but beautiful, and even the most modest plant or animal that managed to survive it was deserving of respect.

Chu came into the open area near where the rock glacier came down from the top. The rocks were well covered in snow, but he knew to be careful. The rocks gave the snow little to hold on to. It was easy to fall.

He saw he was more than halfway over to Soapy's trap line. A dead alder came up on his right and he broke off two switches to use as feelers through the snow.

Chu pushed the switches into the snow to give him feeling as to where the ground was, and what kind of ground it was. He tried to stay just below the rock glacier. This meant navigating among some strange formations, with little cliffs and piles of dirt and snow, pressed against strange, old trees.

The flurries had intensified into a legitimate snowfall and visibility was poor. Chu did not have a good view of the valley, but what he could see around him was beautiful. Every tiny fragment sparkled and danced.

Chu trudged onward, as if entranced by the sound of his own rhythmic footsteps, plunging the stick into the snow ahead of him, then stepping, then driving the stick forward again, then stepping.

When the stick stopped far too soon he was thrown off balance and brought back to his senses. He'd been expecting it to go another two feet further. He stumbled forward to catch himself and saw the snow move underneath where he'd pushed the stick. Even as he regained his balance, he realized the earth was rising up to meet him. Snow flew and, when it fell back to the earth, the form of a bear remained. It was not yet facing him, but it would detect him in just a moment.

Chu realized he had awakened it with the stick. It was confused, angry, and clearly ready to defend itself. Chu meant it no harm, certainly, but he understood that the bear could not know that. It was not about animosity, it was about survival.

Chu tried to untangle himself from the pile of traps he was carrying while doing a quick visual survey of the trees nearby. There was nothing big enough to climb within running distance. He backed up slowly, trying to get out of sight of the beast, knowing that disappearing wasn't as likely as he'd prefer.

He had no luck getting rid of the traps, as they had tangled on his walk, and any movement at all would cause them to clang loudly together and attract the attention of the groggy bear. Chu reached for his knife, pushing the small carcasses roped to his belt to the side. The bear turned around to face Chu, who was standing with legs slightly apart, up to his knees in snow, a pile of metal traps clanging on his shoulder, and a knife in one of his two outstretched hands.

The bear charged at him, angrily plowing through the snow. He stopped just in front of Chu and reared up on his back legs, standing.

Chu was not overwhelmed by fear. When the bear roared, Chu could tell from its rotten teeth that it was very old.

Chu played it by instinct. The old grizzly was angry, too angry for the conventional strategy, to simply lay down and play dead, to be the right move. Chu and the bear lunged at one another simultaneously, Chu leading with his knife, the bear's gaping jaw opened wide, paw drawn back and ready to strike.

At the moment that Chu shoved his knife into the bear's gut, the bear closed her jaws on either side of Chu's large head. She squeezed tightly and lifted him up into the air, pulling Chu's torso upwards, while Chu's knife ripped straight up her belly toward her neck.

Not to be deterred, the bear shook Chu violently while holding his head in her jaws. His temples pulsed as her powerful jaws clenched down on his skull. As he started to fade into unconsciousness, Chu reached up and jammed his knife into the top of her neck. It entered just below her jaw and plunged straight into her throat, then through it, and into her head.

The grizz dropped Chu, and he fell more than his height to the ground, landing on his belly, then sliding a ways down the side of the snowy hill. The snow had picked up considerably, and it was now a blizzard. His unresponsive body stopped sliding. His head was turned sideways and his eyes were open, filling with blood. Chu watched the snow falling, each flake taking on a life of its own, small and precious and wonderful, as he faded into blackness.

53

She stood motionless, on the porch, her mind and her heart drained by the agonizing uncertainty.

Qaniit had run up and down the trail, and did not find Chu. She went to the ridge, and did not find her husband. She returned, her extremities numb from the cold, yet there she remained, on the porch, and there she intended to remain until Chu came home. Or until she knew he wouldn't ever be coming home.

The mounting storm would have alarmed her further had she been capable of perceiving it.

Images from the prior few days rolled through her mind in an endless loop. Maggots crawling on rotting flesh. The hateful expression on her husband's face as he confronted his brother. Chu, willing to take her away, even though she was pregnant with his brother's child. He had to return.

As the blizzard came in, Qaniit swayed in the wind, oblivious to the elements.

He would take care of her. Take her away. For how long had she wanted to leave? Now, once again, she felt like she had for all those years under Kilaun's thumb. Like he was the puppeteer, controlling everything, with everyone under his watch and command. Just as she was slipping out, he would bring her back.

She thought of Chu's sensitivity, and his kindness, and his strength, and his simplicity. And she thought that if her husband ended those things, ended someone so pure, that she would not wait for better things to come in life. She had waited too long for something better. She thought she was not strong enough to have nothing again.

Her hand sat quietly on her stomach. Kilaun's spawn. When she realized she was pregnant, she felt like she was invaded, under siege. It was terrible news, because it tied her further to a man that she wanted no tie to. When Chu told her he would take her away anyway, when he accepted her as she was, Qaniit began to think of it less as an infection and more as a child.

Qaniit had a child many years ago, a boy named Noah. She loved him very much, as she loved the boy's father. When the boy and his father died, she felt like she was turned upside down, and every emotion she had ever had clumsily spilled out of her. When she got up here, and Kilaun took such an interest in her, she did not care enough to say no. She loved him, but he never brought her joy. All the joy she had was used up. It had spilled out back there in the old days, from her old self. This new, hollow person was the one she had lived inside for the better part of a decade. Kilaun controlled the hollow person. She just lived inside its shell, tired.

Chu, in his simplicity, in his plainness, seeing things with the eyes of a child, inspired Qaniit. When she saw things through his eyes, she saw things purely, for what they were. When she saw herself through his eyes, she was beautiful and alive. She was a woman again, not just a human shell.

As the sun set mid-afternoon, the blizzard picked up. She saw a figure entering the town and her heart jumped. It was hard to see through the snow, and she was frozen for what felt like a year as she watched the figure stumble into town.

The wait did not end with what she wanted to see. Her husband, encrusted with snow from head to toe, walked stiffly, slowly toward the house. She ran at him.

"Where is he?"

Kilaun just looked at her, hatefully.

"Where is he?" she yelled, her tears turning on.

He cocked his head.

"Where is your brother?" she sobbed, pushing against him.

He grabbed her wrists with gloved hands and pushed her off of him. She stumbled back and to the ground.

"I have no brother."

And with that, Kilaun continued off toward the house, with no further concern for his wife, who sat on the ground in the snowy street, crying for the man she believed her husband had just killed.

54

Her first question upon Kilaun's return had been about "him." The "him" that wanted to take everything Kilaun had. The "him" that wanted to destroy all Kilaun had created. If there had been any doubt regarding the shift in Qaniit's loyalty, her question resolved it. She had proven herself to be a worthy example of her species. A faithless, weak, and ignoble lot, humans were.

The ridge was for thinking and he had spent much of what little daylight afternoon afforded there, pondering his circumstances. Preparing himself for what needed to be done. The woman had only served to strengthen his resolve. The infection must be cut out, no matter how painful.

When Kilaun arrived a half dozen years ago, he'd found human nature at its worst on display. What little cooperation there had been in the shadow town had broken down by the time he'd reached it. First, there were rival factions, then even those broke down, then it was individuals competing for limited resources.

The ancestors had revealed to him how it could be done, how he could expand the resources, making enough for all.

There had been skepticism. Some of them had been there for many years and did not trust anyone new, from down south or not. The thing that was said most often was, "This valley will *not* support a town." This was the thing that everyone believed, so they focused their efforts on not dying until they could leave. They'd figured he was just there to rule over them, or to take what was theirs. But he was faithful to his mission, faithful to the vision he'd been granted. He built them a place where one could lead a life worth living and, one by one, they had come around.

And they were thriving, wretched though they were, thriving in spite of themselves, here, in the place he had crafted for them with the help of the ancestors.

He had gone to the mountains and caught three dall sheep. It took him a month, but he managed it. And he brought them down to the town and set to domesticate them. The townspeople thought he was crazy. He believed that domestication was the key to their success. It just so happened that he was right. In a handful of years, he built the town from a bunch of people devoting all of their efforts into putting food in their stomachs into people with leisure time, so that they could have a man dedicated to lumber work and another dedicated to machinery. This was something. It was an accomplishment. It was far more than the other villages had managed in such a short time.

Kilaun had built it. He had given everything he had to it.

Until Chu. Chu came, came to take his wife, came to take possession of the place he'd built, to release his prisoner, and perhaps even to take his life. None of the people Kilaun had delivered to a better existence came to his aid. All he'd done was seemingly forgotten. Perhaps the ancestors also wished for Kilaun to see this, to see the ways of men, so that he might understand when he joined the ancestors when his work was done.

And history had started to repeat itself so quickly, the town first dividing into factions. The disintegration would continue if Kilaun didn't act. So act he would. It was his duty. His duty to the town he'd built, his duty as a husband and his duty to the ancestors. Kilaun had sacrificed so much for this town and the ancestors had told him that he had another sacrifice to make.

He didn't relish the task. But he did not shirk from it either. This was what it meant to be responsible, to do the right thing, to rise above. The will of the ancestors would be done.

That thought gave Kilaun peace. The ancestors approved of this. He was but the tool bringing it about. And being at peace for the first time in a good while, he became hungry. He went into the oddly quiet kitchen and found a pot of stew on the stove. He ate voraciously. And, when his stomach was full, he slept. Trekking through the blizzard had been taxing.

With the decision to dispatch his brother made, with the approval from the ancestors, he slept deeply, straight through until morning.

He awakened feeling refreshed, vigorous, full of purpose. He woke when his body chose, not when the surly cook decided to bother him.

It occurred to him that having slept through the night might've meant that his wife never joined him. She'd been upset yesterday, but that was often the case. Her moods were unpredictable and of little consequence. But she was pregnant! That was a truly excellent thing!

He ambled lightly downstairs, wearing only house pants. Chena was in the kitchen.

"Good morning," she said, nervously. This was the first time in years that she had not assaulted him with a barrage of complaints upon his waking. She set a plate of food in front of him on the center island.

"Where's my wife?" he asked.

"I–. I don't know."

He took a bite. Ready to eat again, even after eating so much last night.

"What of Chu? Where is he?"

"I don't know, Sir."

"Sir?"

He looked up at the old woman. She'd been intently scrubbing the same spot on the counter since she'd put his breakfast in front of him. If it had been dirty, it certainly wasn't now. She was avoiding eye contact. She didn't want to talk to him. She knew something.

"What's going on, Chena?" he asked.

"What do you mean?" she responded. The words were on her tongue before he'd even said anything, it seemed, as though she were waiting for him to ask.

"Tell me why you're trying to avoid looking at me." He paused to allow her a moment to comply, but she said nothing.

"And why you're speaking to me so strangely." This was said as he rose from his chair.

This woman, he had known her for years. She should know better than to keep things from him. He felt anger rising within him, and the anger fed upon itself, he became more angry at her for ruining his good mood. He had never had he seen her display such a degree of nervousness. He approached her and she tensed.

He spoke her name in a very firm voice. A voice he knew was intimidating. A voice bearing a trace of anger. "Chena." When she failed to respond he moved directly behind her, behind her and to the right.

"Chena. You will tell me what you know." Again, nothing.

"You *will* tell me."

Kilaun brought his fist down on the counter hard. "*NOW!*" Chena jumped, more than you'd expect an old woman to, and it seemed as though twenty sentences attempted to expel themselves from her mouth simultaneously. She was jabbering and he could only make out some of it, the words made sense, but not together, not in the sequence she was using them. Qaniit, guns, the ridge, Qaniit, the porch, Chu, traps, Soapy, blizzard.

"*STOP!*" he roared.

She silenced herself.

"Take a deep breath," he instructed. Chena complied. "Now, please start at the beginning, but calm down, go slowly, and be clear."

"Did you kill Chu?" she asked, fear in her eyes.

"No! What?! Why would you ask that?"

"Qaniit thinks you did."

"Oh, well, she is wrong. I haven't." He pause, then continued, "But I will."

He looked at the old cook, who looked down and to the side, and everywhere but back at him. He took a step back, no longer needing to intimidate her.

"Chena, I'm going to explain something to you. I made this town what it is and it is my duty to preserve it. Chu came and sought to destroy it, sought to destroy me. You saw how he behaved toward my wife. You saw how he attempted to undermine me in front of the entire village. I do not know why he chose to behave as he did. But I am committed to this village, and I will not allow anyone, even if he calls himself my brother, to tear it down."

He paused, weighing his words. "The ancestors have led the way, and they lead the way in this as well. I have asked him to leave us, and he has refused."

The old woman was clearly not going to speak again. Kilaun had said what he had to and was tired of explaining himself to people who weren't capable of comprehending what true responsibility meant.

As he returned to the table, he added "Chena, you are not to speak of this until after I've done what I have to do." He grabbed his unfinished plate of food and went to the porch to eat and look at his town.

There'd been a good snow last night. After it snowed, things seemed peaceful, quieter, cleaner. He did not care about the cold, and he put his bare feet square on the floor timbers and his bare back right against the logs on the side of the house. It always felt warmer when it snowed. As if the snow absorbed the coldness.

Things would be much better between him and Qaniit without Chu around. And a family! They would be a family. That would make her happy, something to care for, to care about. He imagined he would be granted a son.

This, this was the fruition of all he'd worked for. Creating the village was creating a future, but Kilaun knew he would join the ancestors someday. And now there would be someone to remain. Someone to carry on the legacy, someone raised to know of the ancestors, to know how to listen to them.

As he chewed his fried bread, Kilaun heard the sound of a horse's footfalls in the snow. He stood up and went to the end of the porch. It was Buck, of course, standing there, dumbly, outside the stable. The horse was loose, and Qaniit was not in sight. It was curious. Kilaun trotted across the snow with bare feet to see about the horse.

Buck was obviously cold. He was shivering and desperate to get in the warm stable. Kilaun slid the door open and brought him in. As he took the blankets off the horse, he saw a note pinned on. He unfolded it and read –

Good for you. You got what you wanted. Where are the ancestors now? You took away the only thing I was looking forward to. By the time you get this, we'll be even.

They had said she would kill his child.

Kilaun dropped the note. Eyes closed, he staggered back two steps, as though struck in the chest by a heavy blow.

She had done it. She would not have his child.

Why had they not said she would hurt herself?

Tears formed in his eyes. He dropped to a knee, head falling into his hands.

He would have stopped her. He could have done something. They had not told him. She was gone.

He had done everything they asked of him. He had devoted his life to their wishes. Was this to be his reward?

They had betrayed him. They, too, were faithless. His brother. His wife. The ancestors.

The bitter tears stung his eyes. He was alone. He had nothing. His wife would rather die than give him a child. The ancestors had deceived him. For how long had they been doing so?

How had she done it? He pictured her throwing herself into an icy river. There was one a couple miles west that was too fast to freeze. He thought of the baby in his dream, choking and drowning and unable to right itself. His son. His son. He was responsible. It was no better than if he'd done it by his own hands.

Kilaun was human. Like the rest. Weak, faithless, gullible. He who would have killed his own brother. He had not even done it, yet he had been punished beyond measure.

As Kilaun, now curled on the floor of the stable, wept. He imagined the ancestors. How they laughed at the grand joke they'd played. How he hated them.

*

Kilaun didn't remember rising from the floor, nor building a fire for the horse, nor walking back to the house in his bare feet. He didn't recall his matter-of-factly telling Chena that his wife and brother were dead. These were small mercies. Whatever his faults, Kilaun had suffered much.

He enlisted the help of the men in town, and they helped him search for the bodies of his wife and brother. The cook's son came back telling of the scene up on the ridge where it looked like Chu had gotten in trouble. He took Kilaun up there to a bloody mess in the snow. It was the scene of a grand battle and Kilaun was proud of his brother. Now that was a grand way to die, fighting a wild creature in the wild mountains. The snow told the story that Chu would never get to tell. And, even though he hadn't won, the snow told the story that Chu had put up a hell of a fight.

They never found Qaniit's body. There were tracks over by the partially frozen river out west, but even those were nearly useless with the snow that had come in. But they confirmed Kilaun's suspicion that this is where she went. She had wanted to escape him and she managed that.

Kilaun did not go up to the ridge to seek counsel anymore. Instead, he spent his time thinking about smaller things. He doubted whether the ancestors ever spoke to him at all, or if he had just been thrown up into the air, floating like a leaf, happening to land in this village. It wasn't much, but at least it was a place. Their place. And this thought comforted Kilaun as he waited out the rest of winter just like the rest of them. Just like a regular human.

55

Leif and Libby waited out the snow in the tiny island paradise of his cabin. The topic of spring was largely avoided. Leif was quite fond of his new companion and feared her departure. Libby, for her part, found that Leif was surprisingly competent at nearly everything, knowledgeable about just as much, and he even had a sense of humor when she got him talking. She trusted him more completely than she had trusted anyone in a very long time.

After less than a month in the cabin, they had an awkward exchange that was more stammering than conversation, where it was agreed that it was impractical for either of them to sleep downstairs on the palette. Sharing warmth and blankets in a winter like this was, well, vital to conservation and the general efficiency of a remote household. The conversation ended with both parties trying to hide broad smiles.

But the topic of spring could not be avoided forever, and it had been on Libby's mind as well as Leif's. Being so near the town had weighed on Libby, who did not trust the townspeople to continue to accept her freedom. Call them old wounds, but she worried they would decide she was a threat again.

Leif wasn't particularly keen on the idea of going Outside, so he found himself with a decision to make.

When Tali came out to tell them what had happened in town, she also let them know that the government they'd called a Minarchy in the south had fallen. Although Libby had technically been a representative of it, she did not find herself much affected by the news. Certainly, her sorrow on hearing about Qaniit and Chu was greater.

Leif grew very quiet in the days following Tali's arrival. Libby tried to give him his space, to let him mourn in his own way. When he was himself again, she found his reluctance to leaving his home lessened.

They decided not to travel south. Libby wanted to be away from the village that had imprisoned her, but was concerned she'd be just as poorly received in the south for having worked with and for the previous government. Plus, even if Leif did prefer anarchy to the more reputable forms of government, they figured the mainland wouldn't make for the quiet life to which they had become accustomed.

Instead, they set out north before the snow melted toward the lowlands. They'd constructed sleds for the horses to pull. The new horse was called Sam and he took well to work. Still, they traveled light, with just 150 pounds of supplies – 15 pounds of live chickens, 50 pounds of tools, 30 pounds of food, and miscellaneous provisions like buckets, clothes, and dishes. Paring down everything they needed for a whole new life wasn't easy, but they had a good few months of winter during which to do it.

One of the other tidbits that Tali had passed on when she came by was that Kilaun had been "reborn." He was apparently so distraught over his brother and wife that he went on a quest into the mountains, for three days and nights, and performed some ancient rites that he said were passed down to him from his people. When he returned, he claimed to have gained a profound understanding of morality, one that required him to acknowledge the saving power of the Lord Jesus Christ. He suddenly turned preacher and set to convincing the entire town to convert to Protestantism. The townspeople felt bad enough for him to humor him, promising to build a church come spring.

Shortly before Leif and Libby left for the pass, Leif went into town to say goodbye to Tali (and, undeniably, to steal Buck back) and saw that they really had begun construction on a church, using some of the wood from the old mill building. "Well, I'll be," escaped his lips. Leif invited Tali to come along on their journey, but she had found a bit more happiness in recent months, having taken on the task of schooling the very few local children who were of age to learn.

Leif and Libby made good headway in the first day, nearly ten miles, before they entered territory that Leif had never seen before. The following day, the mountains opened on either side of them, leaving them on a wide-open glacier. They navigated the crevasses as carefully as they could until they reached a flat ice field. They could see many miles in every direction.

"You sure we didn't take a wrong turn?" Libby joked, her lips already cracked from the sun, wind, and cold.

"I reckon we got three more days to go," Leif responded. Only a few people had crossed this way over the years, but at least it was crossable. On the far side were the lowlands that didn't promise much of anything except change. That was good enough for both of them.

They sat on that vast expanse of ice and watched the sky open up overhead. It made them feel so small, and so free.

"I can't believe we live like this," Libby said, her voice full of wonder.

He spent the next minute taking it all in, trying to see it through her eyes, still new to this place.

Finally, Leif sighed, "Guess this is all that living is," and he reached over to pull Libby closer.

SUMMER

In the mountains of Alaska, there is no spring. There is only summer and winter, and one pushes into the other with no appreciation for gradual change.

This particular summer began the way all Alaskan summers do, with a dog laying in the center of a small mountain town, baking in the alien sun, oblivious to the world around him. Gun couldn't be happier that winter had passed, that the mud from melt had dried up, and that here he was to relish the first summer day.

Gun still stayed with Tali some days, for old times sake, but he had started sleeping at the big house far more often. Kilaun, in his loneliness, had taken to caring for the old dog, and taking care of him well at that. Gun was given more than enough food, constant attention, and even the occasional bath. The man had not always been so nice, but Gun figured it was in his own best interest to forgive him.

In his younger days, Gun had been a sled dog. He reflected on those days only in his dreams. In those dreams, he was in the pack, running with all his might, pulling and straining and pushing himself to his limit. He enjoyed the dreams, but he was happy to have a warm bed and meat and affection in his old age. Summers were always a break for sled dogs anyway. This one wouldn't be much different from those of his youth.

Gun kept to himself when he was not escorting Kilaun up to the ridge, or out to the spring, or guarding him in the office. On those afternoons when the dog traveled solo, he would wander around town, check on the townspeople and see who wanted some company or who had food to spare, or he would lay in the square as he did on this particular day.

One day when Gun was exploring up near the toe, he stopped by Leif's cabin. He found no one there, save for a lone chicken who must have been left behind. Given his dedication to maintaining the natural balance of the ecosystem, he promptly dispatched the chicken, feeling self-satisfied for having done so.

When Gun reflected on the previous winter, he found it not much different than any of the dozen winters he had so far enjoyed. It was the winter in which he got the porcupine quills, but this was not the first time that had happened, just the worst. It was by no means the most significant of his winters, just one of the longer ones. Humans staying, humans going, humans trying to figure out something better for themselves.

Gun hoped to keep the humans company for another winter, but he wasn't particularly worried about it. He was the only resident of the village with the unique disposition of being able to live each day as if it were his last.

As luck would have it, Kilaun went down to the Port that summer and brought back a companion for Gun. She was a small thing, and rather obnoxious at that, but the man seemed to think she would turn into a fine companion. Gun did not mind the company, either of the pup or the man who seemed to have softened considerably despite the long winter.

THE END

www.ingramcontent.com/pod-product-compliance
Lightning Source LLC
Chambersburg PA
CBHW031252170626
46807CB00001B/98